CHRISTMAS
WITH HER
SECRET PRINCE

CHRISTMAS WITH HER SECRET PRINCE

NINA SINGH

MILLS & BOON

First published in Great Britain 2018
by Mills & Boon, an imprint of HarperCollins*Publishers*
1 London Bridge Street, London, SE1 9GF

Large Print edition 2019

© 2018 Nilay Nina Singh

ISBN: 978-0-263-08213-5

MIX
Paper from
responsible sources
FSC C007454

This book is produced from independently certified FSC™ paper to ensure responsible forest management. For more information visit www.harpercollins.co.uk/green.

Printed and bound in Great Britain
by CPI Group (UK) Ltd, Croydon, CR0 4YY

To my two very own princes.

And my two princesses.

CHAPTER ONE

Prince Rayhan al Saibbi was not looking forward to his next meeting. In fact, he was dreading it. After all, it wasn't often he went against his father—the man who also happened to be king of Verdovia.

But it had to be done. This might very well be his last chance to exert any kind of control over his own life. Even if it was to be only a temporary respite. Fate had made him prince of Verdovia. And his honor-bound duty to that fate would come calling soon enough. He just wanted to try and bat it away one last time.

The sun shone bright and high over the majestic mountain range outside his window. A crisp blue stream meandered along its base. The pleasant sunny day meant his father would most likely be enjoying his breakfast on the patio off the four-seasons room in the east wing.

Rayhan found his father sitting at the far end

of the table. Piles of papers and a sleek new laptop were mixed in with various plates of fruits and pastries. A twinge of guilt hit Rayhan as he approached. The king never stopped working. For that matter, neither did the queen, his mother. A fact that needed to be addressed after the events of the past year. Part of the reason Rayhan was in his current predicament.

This conversation wasn't going to be easy. His father had been king for a long time. He was used to making the rules and expected everyone to follow them. Particularly when it came to his son.

But these days the king wasn't thinking entirely straight. Motivated by an alarming health scare Rayhan's mother had experienced a few months back and prompted by the troublesome maneuverings of a disagreeable council member, his father had decided that the royal family needed to strengthen and reaffirm their stability. Unfortunately, he'd also decided that Rayhan would be the primary vehicle to cement that stability.

His father motioned for him to be seated when he saw Rayhan approach.

"Thank you for seeing me, Father. I know how busy you are."

His father nodded. "It sounded urgent based on your messages. What can I assist you with, son? Dare I hope you're closer to making a decision?"

"I am. Just not in the way you might assume."

Rayhan focused his gaze on his father's face. A face that could very well be an older version of his own. Dark olive skin with high cheekbones and ebony eyes.

"I don't understand," his father began. "You were going to spend some time with the ladies in consideration. Then you were to make a choice."

Rayhan nodded. "I've spent time with all three of them, correct. They're all lovely ladies, Father. Very accomplished—all of them stunning and impressive in their own unique way. You have chosen well."

"They come from three of the most notable and prominent families of our land. You marrying a prominent daughter of Verdovia will go far to address our current problems."

"Like I said, you have chosen well."

The king studied him. "Then what appears to be the issue?"

Where to start? First of all, he wasn't ready to be wedded to any of the ladies in question. In fact, he wasn't ready to be wedded at all.

But he had a responsibility. Both to his family and to the kingdom.

"Perhaps I shall choose for you," the king suggested, his annoyance clear as the crisp morning air outside. "You know how important this is. And how urgent. Councilman Riza is preparing a resolution as we speak to propose studying the efficacy and necessity of the royal family's very existence."

"You know it won't go anywhere. He's just stirring chaos."

"I despise chaos." His father blew out a deep breath. "All the more reason to put this plan into action, son."

The *plan* his father referred to meant the end of Rayhan's life as he knew it. "It just seems such an archaic and outdated method. A bachelor prince choosing from qualified ladies to serve as his queen when he eventually ascends the throne."

His father shrugged. "Arranged marriages are quite common around the world. Particularly for a young man of your standing. Global alliances are regularly formed through marriage vows. It's how your mother and I wedded, as you know. These ladies I have chosen are very well-known and popular in the kingdom."

Rayhan couldn't argue the point. There was the talented prima ballerina who had stolen the people's hearts when she'd first appeared on stage several years ago. Then there was the humanitarian who'd made the recent influx of refugees and their plight her driving cause. And finally, a councilman's beautiful daughter, who also happened to be an international fashion model.

Amazing ladies. All of whom seemed to be approaching the king's proposition more as a career opportunity than anything else. Which in blatant terms was technically correct. Of course, the people didn't know that fact. They just believed their crown prince to be linked to three different ladies, and rumors abounded that he would propose to one of them within weeks. A well-calculated palace publicity stunt.

"As far as being outdated," the king continued, "have you seen the most popular show in America these days? It involves an eligible bachelor choosing from among several willing ladies. By giving them weekly roses, of all things." His father barked out a laugh at the idea.

"But this isn't some reality show," Rayhan argued. "This is my life."

"Nevertheless, a royal wedding will distract from this foolishness of Riza's."

Rayhan couldn't very well argue that point either. The whole kingdom was even now in the frenzied midst of preparing for the wedding of the half century, everyone anxious to see which young lady the prince would choose for himself. Combined with the festivities of the holiday season, the level of excitement and celebration throughout the land was almost palpable.

And Rayhan was about to go and douse it all like a wet blanket over a warming fire.

Bah humbug.

Well, so be it. This was his life they were talking about. He wanted to claim one last bit of it. He wouldn't take no for an answer. Not this time. But this was a new experience for him. Rayhan had never actually willingly gone against the king's wishes before. Not for something this important anyway.

"Well, I've come to a different decision," he told his father. Rayhan made sure to look him straight in the eye as he continued, "I've decided to wait."

The king blinked. Several times. Rapidly. "I beg your pardon?"

"I'd like to hold off. I'm not ready to choose a fiancée. Not just yet."

"You can only postpone for so long, son. The kingdom is waiting for a royal wedding… We have announced your intention to marry. And then there's your mother."

Rayhan felt a pang of guilt through his chest at the mention of the queen. She'd given them all quite a scare last year. "Mother is fine now."

"Still, she needs to slow down. I won't have her health jeopardized again. Someone needs to help take over some of the queen's regular duties. Your sisters are much too young."

"All I'm asking for is some time, Father. Perhaps we can come to a compromise."

The king leaned toward him, his arms resting on the table. At least he was listening. "What sort of compromise did you have in mind?"

Rayhan cleared his throat and began to tell him.

"Honestly, Mel. If you handle that invitation any more, it's going to turn into ash in your hands."

Melinda Osmon startled as her elderly, matronly employer walked by the counter where she sat waiting for her shift to begin. The older woman was right. This had to be at least the fifth or sixth time Mel had taken the stationery out simply to stare at it since it had arrived in her mailbox several days ago.

The Honorable Mayor and Mrs. Spellman request the pleasure of your presence...

"You caught me," Mel replied, swiftly wiping the moisture off her cheeks.

"Just send in your reply already," Greta added, her back turned to her as she poured coffee for the customer sitting at the end of the counter. The full breakfast crowd wasn't due in for another twenty minutes or so. "Then figure out what you're going to wear."

Melinda swallowed past the lump in her throat before attempting an answer. "Greta, you know I can't go this year. It's just not worth the abject humiliation."

Greta turned to her so fast that some of the coffee splashed out of her coffeepot. "Come again? What in the world do you have to be humiliated about?"

Not this again. Greta didn't seem to understand, nor did she want to. How about the fact that Mel hadn't yet moved on? Unlike her ex-husband. The ex-husband who would be at the same party with his fashionable, svelte and beautiful new fiancée. "Well, for one thing, I'd be going solo. That's humiliating enough in itself."

Greta jutted out her chin and snapped her gum loudly. "And why is that? You're not the one who behaved shamefully and had the affair. That scoundrel you were married to should be the one feeling too ashamed to show his face at some fancy-schmancy party you both used to attend every year when you were man and wife."

Mel cringed at the unfiltered description.

"Now, you listen to me, young lady—"

Luckily, another customer cleared his throat just then, clearly impatient for a hit of caffeine. Greta humphed and turned away to pour. Mel knew the reprieve would be short-lived. Greta had very strong opinions about how Mel should move along into the next chapter of her life. She also had very strong opinions about Mel's ex. To say the older woman was outraged on Mel's behalf was to put it mildly. In fact, the only person who might be even angrier was Greta's even older sister, Frannie. Not that Mel wasn't pretty outraged herself. A lot of good that did for her, though. Strong emotions were not going to get her a plus-one to the mayor's Christmas soiree. And she certainly was nowhere near ready to face the speculation and whispery gossip that was sure to greet her if she set foot in that ballroom alone.

"She's right, you know," Frannie announced, sliding into the seat next to Mel. The two sisters owned the Bean Pot Diner on Marine Street in the heart of South Boston. The only place that would hire her when she'd found herself broke, alone and suddenly separated. "I hate to admit when that blabbermouth is right but she sure is about this. You should go to that party and enjoy yourself. Show that no-good, cheating charlatan that you don't give a damn what he thinks."

"I don't think I have it in me, Frannie. Just to show up and then have to stare at Eric and his fiancée having the time of their lives, while I'll be sitting there all alone."

"I definitely don't think you should do that."

Well, that was a sudden change of position, Melinda thought, eyeing her friend. "So you agree I shouldn't go?"

"No, that's not what I said. I think you should go, look ravishing and then confront him about all he put you through. Then demand that he return your money."

Melinda sighed. She should have seen that argument coming. "First of all, I gave him that money." Foolishly. The hard-earned money that her dear parents had left her after their deaths. It was supposed to have been an investment in Eric's future. Their future. She had gladly handed it to him to help him get through dental school. Then it was supposed to be her turn to make some kind of investment in herself while he supported her. Instead, he'd left her for his perky, athletic dental assistant. His much younger, barely-out-of-school dental assistant. And now they happily cared for teeth together during the day, while planning an extravagant wedding in their off-hours. "I gave it to him with no strings attached."

"And you should take him to court to get some of it back!" Frannie slapped her palm against the counter. Greta sashayed back over to where the two of them sat.

"That's right," Greta declared. "You should go to that damn party looking pretty as a fashion model. Then demand he pay you back. Every last cent. Or you'll see him in front of a judge."

Mel sighed and bit down on the words that were forming on her tongue. As much as she longed to tell the two women to mind their own business, Mel just couldn't bring herself to do it. They'd been beyond kind to her when she'd needed it the most. Not to mention, they were the closest thing to family Mel could count since her divorce a year ago.

"How? I barely have the money for court fees. Let alone any to hire an attorney."

"Then start with the party," Greta declared as her sister nodded enthusiastically. "At the very least, ruin his evening. Show him what he's missing out on."

Nothing like a couple of opinionated matrons double-teaming you.

Mel let out an unamused laugh. "As if. I don't even have a dress to wear. I sold all my fancier clothes just to make rent that first month."

Greta waved a hand in dismissal. "So buy another one. I tell you, if I had your figure and that great dark hair of yours, I'd be out shopping right now. Women like you can find even the highest-end clothing on sale."

Mel ignored the compliment. "I can't even afford the stuff on sale these days, Greta."

"So take an advance on your paycheck," Frannie offered from across the counter. "We know you're good for it."

Mel felt the immediate sting of tears. These women had taken her in when she'd needed friendship and support the most. She'd never be able to repay their kindness. She certainly had no desire to take advantage of it. "I can't ask you to do that for me, ladies."

"Nonsense," they both said in unison.

"You'd be doing it for us," Greta added.

"For you?"

"Sure. Let two old bats like us live vicariously through you. Go to that ball and then come back and tell us all about it."

Frannie nodded in agreement. "That's right. Especially the part about that no-good scoundrel begging you for forgiveness after he takes one look at ya."

Mel smiled in spite of herself. These two certainly knew how to cook up a good fantasy. Eric had left her high and dry and never looked back even once. As far as fantasies went, she was more likely to turn a frog into a prince than receive any kind of apology from her ex-husband.

"I don't think that's going to happen anytime soon." Or ever. Mel reached down to tighten the laces of her comfortable white tennis shoes. She had a very long shift ahead of her, starting with the breakfast crowd and ending with the early-evening dinner guests.

"You won't know unless you go to this ball."

She couldn't even tell which of the ladies had thrown that out. Mel sighed and straightened to look at them both. Her bosses might look like gentle, sweet elderly ladies, complete with white hair done up in buns, but they could be relentless once they set their minds to something.

"All right. I give."

They both squealed with delight. "Then it's settled," Frannie declared and clasped her hands in front of her chest.

Mel held a hand up. "Not so fast. I haven't agreed to go just yet."

Greta's smile faded. "Come again?"

"How about a deal?"

"What kind of deal?"

"I'll go out after my shift and look for a dress." Though how she would summon the energy after such a long day was a mystery. But she was getting the feeling she'd hear about this all day unless she threw her two bosses some kind of bone. "If, and only if, I come across a dress that's both affordable and appropriate, I'll reconsider going."

Frannie opened her mouth, clearly about to protest. Mel cut her off.

"It's my only offer. Take it or leave it."

"Fine," they both said in unison before turning away. Mel stood just as the bell for the next order up rang from the kitchen. She had a long day ahead of her and it was only just starting. She was a waitress now. Not the young bride of an up-and-coming urban dentist who attended fancy holiday balls and went shopping for extravagant ball gowns. That might have been her reality once, but it had been short-lived.

Little did the Perlman sisters know, she had told them something of a fib just now when making that deal. She had no expectation that she'd find any kind of dress that would merit attending that party in a week.

The chances were slim to zero.

His driver-slash-security-guard—who also happened to be a dear childhood friend—was very unhappy with him at the moment. Rayhan ignored the scowl of the other man as he watched the streets of downtown Boston outside his passenger-side window. Every shop front had been decorated with garlands and glittery Christmas decorations. Bright lights were strung on everything from the lamp poles to shop windows. Let his friend scowl away, Rayhan thought. He was going to go ahead and enjoy the scenery. But when Saleh took yet another turn a little too fast and sharp, he found he'd had enough. Saleh was acting downright childish.

To top it off, they appeared to be lost. Saleh had refused to admit he needed the assistance of the navigation system and now they appeared to be nowhere near their destination.

"You know you didn't have to come," Rayhan reminded the other man. "You volunteered, remember?"

Saleh grunted. "I clearly wasn't thinking straight. Why are we here, again? At this particular time, no less."

"You know this."

"I know you're delaying the inevitable."

He was right, of course. Not that Rayhan was

going to admit it out loud. "I still have a bit of time to live my life as I see fit."

"And you decided you needed to do part of that in Boston?"

Rayhan shrugged, resuming his perusal of the outside scenery. "That was completely co-incidental. My father's been eyeing property out here for months now. Perfect opportunity for me to come find a prime location and seal the deal."

"Yes, so you say. It's a way to… How do the Americans say it? To kill two birds with one stone?"

"Precisely."

"So why couldn't you have come out here with the new soon-to-be-princess after your engagement?"

Rayhan pinched the bridge of his nose. "I just needed to get away before it all gets out of con-trol, Saleh. I don't expect you to understand."

Not many people would, Rayhan thought. Particularly not his friend, who had married the grade-school sweetheart he'd been in love with since their teen years. Unlike Rayhan, Saleh didn't have to answer to nor appease a whole country when it came to his choice of bride.

Rayhan continued, "Everywhere I turn in Verdovia, I'm reminded of the upcoming ceremonies. Everyone is completely preoccupied with who the heir will choose to marry, what the wedding will be like. Yada yada. There are odds being placed in every one of our island casinos on everything from the identity of the next queen to what flavor icing will adorn the royal wedding cake."

Saleh came to a sudden halt at a red light, a wide grin spread across his face.

"What?" Rayhan asked.

"I placed my wager on the vanilla buttercream."

"I see. That's good to know." He made a mental note to go with anything but the vanilla buttercream when the time came. If he had any say on the matter, that was. Between his mother and the princess-to-be, he'd likely have very little sway in such decisions. No doubt his shrewd friend had made his bet based on the very same assumption.

"I don't understand why you refuse to simply

embrace your fate, my friend. You're the heir of one of the most powerful men in the world. With that comes the opportunity to marry and gain a beautiful, accomplished lady to warm your bed. There are worse things in life."

Saleh overlooked the vast amount of responsibility that came with such a life. The stability and prosperity of a whole kingdom full of people would fall on Rayhan's shoulders as soon as he ascended. Even more so than it did now. Few people could understand the overwhelming prospect of such a position. As far as powerful, how much did any of that mean when even your choice of bride was influenced by the consideration of your position?

"How easy for you to say," he told Saleh just as the light turned green and they moved forward. "You found a beautiful woman who you somehow tricked into thinking marrying you was a good idea."

Saleh laughed with good-natured humor. "The greatest accomplishment of my life."

Rayhan was about to answer when a screeching noise jolted both men to full alert. A cyclist veered toward their vehicle at an alarming speed. Saleh barely had time to turn the wheel in order to avoid a full-on collision. Unfortunately, the cyclist shifted direction at precisely the same time. Both he and their SUV were now heading the same way. Right toward a pedestrian. Saleh hit the brakes hard. Rayhan gripped the side bar, waiting for the inevitable impact. Fortunately for them, it never came.

The cyclist, however, kept going. And, unfortunately for the poor pedestrian woman, the bicycle ran straight into her, knocking her off her feet.

"Watch where you're going!" the rider shouted back over his shoulder, not even bothering to stop.

Rayhan immediately jumped out of the car. He ran around to the front of the SUV and knelt down where the woman still lay by the sidewalk curb.

"Miss, are you all right?"

A pair of startled eyes met his. Very bright green eyes. They reminded him of the shimmering stream that lay outside his windows back home. Not that this was any sort of time to notice that kind of thing.

She blinked, rubbing a hand down a cheek that was rapidly bruising even as they spoke. Saleh appeared at his side.

"Is she okay?"

"I don't know. She's not really responding. Miss, are you all right?"

Her eyes grew wide as she looked at him. "You're lovely," she said in a low, raspy voice.

Dear heavens. The woman clearly had some kind of head injury. "We have to get you to a doctor."

Saleh swore beside him. "I'm so terribly sorry, miss. I was trying to avoid the bike and the cyclist was trying to avoid me but he turned right toward you—"

The woman was still staring at Rayhan. She didn't acknowledge Saleh nor his words at all.

He had a sudden urge to hold her, to comfort her. He wanted to wrap her in his arms, even though she was a complete stranger.

Rayhan reached for his cell phone. "I'll call for an ambulance."

The woman gave a shake of her head before he could dial. "No. I'm okay. Just a little shaken." She blinked some more and looked around. Her eyes seemed to regain some focus. Rayhan allowed himself a breath of relief. Maybe she'd be all right. Her next words brought that hopeful thought to a halt.

"My dress. Do you see it?"

Did she think somehow her clothes had been knocked off her upon impact? "You…uh…you are wearing it still."

Her gaze scanned the area where she'd fallen. "No. See, I found one. I didn't think I would. But I did. And it wasn't all that pricey."

Rayhan didn't need to hear any more. Unless she was addled to begin with, which could very well be a possibility, the lady had clearly suffered a blow to the head. To top it all off, they were blocking traffic and drawing a crowd. Kneeling closer to the woman sprawled in front of him, he lifted her gently into his arms and then stood. "Let's get you to a hospital."

"Oh!" she cried out as Rayhan walked back toward the SUV with her embraced against his chest.

Saleh was fast on his heels and opening the passenger door for them. "No, see, it's all right," she began to protest. "I don't need a doctor. Just that gown."

"We'll make sure to get you a dress," Rayhan reassured her, trying to tell her what she clearly needed to hear. Why was she so focused on clothing at a time like this? "Right after a doctor takes a look at you."

He gently deposited her in the back seat, then sat down next to her. "No, wait," she argued. "I don't need a doctor. I just want my dress."

But Saleh was already driving toward a hospital.

The woman took a panicked look out the window and then winced. The action must have hurt her injuries somehow. She touched a shaky finger to her cheek, which was now a dark purple, surrounded by red splotches.

Even in the messy state she was in, he couldn't help but notice how striking her features were. Dark, thick waves of black hair escaped the confines of some sort of complicated bun on top of her head. A long slender neck graced her slim shoulders. She was curvy—not quite what one would consider slim. Upon first glance, he would never consider someone like her his "type," so to speak. But he had to admit, he appreciated her rather unusual beauty.

That choice of words had him uncomfortably shifting in his seat. He stole a glance at her as she explored her facial injuries with shaky fingers.

Now her right eye had begun to swell as an angry, dark circular ring developed around it. Rayhan bit out a sharp curse. Here he was trying to enjoy what could very well be his last trip to the United States as a free man and he'd ended up hurting some poor woman on his first day here.

Perhaps Saleh was right. Maybe this whole trip had been a terrible idea. Maybe he should have just stayed home and accepted his fate.

There was at least one person who would be much better off right now if he had.

CHAPTER TWO

SHE WOULD HAVE been much better off if she'd just ignored that blasted invitation and thrown it away as soon as it arrived in her mailbox. She should have never even opened it and she definitely should have never even considered going to that godforsaken party. Her intuition had been right from the beginning. She no longer had any kind of business attending fancy balls and wearing glamorous gowns.

But no, she had to go and indulge two little old ladies, as well as her own silly whim. Look where that had got her—sitting on an exam table in a cold room at Mass General, with a couple of strange men out in the hallway.

Although they had to be the best-looking strangers she'd ever encountered. Particularly the one who had carried her to the car. She studied him now through the small window of her exam room door. He stood leaning against the wall, patiently waiting for the doctor to come examine her.

Even in her stunned shock while she lay sprawled by the side of the road, she hadn't been able to help but notice the man's striking good looks. Dark haired, with the barest shadow of a goatee, he looked like he could have stepped out of a cologne advertisement. Though there was no way he was some kind of male fashion model. He carried himself with much too much authority.

His eyes were dark as charcoal, his skin tone just on the darker side of dessert tan. Even before they'd spoken, she'd known he wasn't local.

His looks had taken her by surprise, or perhaps it had been the blow she'd suffered, but she distinctly remembered thinking he was lovely.

Which was a downright silly thought. A better description would be to say he looked dangerous.

Mel shook off the fanciful thoughts. She had other things to worry about besides the striking good looks of the man who had brought her here. They'd called the diner after she'd been processed. Presumably, either Greta or Frannie was on her way to join her at the hospital now. Mel felt a slight pang of guilt about one of them having to leave in the middle of closing up the diner for the night.

She would have frowned but it hurt too much. Her face had taken the brunt of the collision with the reckless cyclist, who, very rudely, had continued on his way. At least the two gentlemen out there hadn't left her alone and bleeding by the side of the road. Though now that meant she would be saddled with an ER bill she couldn't afford. Thinking about that expense, coupled with what she'd paid for the evening dress, had her eyes stinging with regret. In all the confusion and chaos right after the accident, her shopping bag had been left behind. Mel knew she should be grateful that the accident hadn't been worse, but she couldn't help but feel sorry for herself. Would she ever catch a break?

A sharp knock on the door was quickly followed by the entrance of a harried-looking doctor. He did a bit of a double take when he saw her face.

"Let's take a look at you, Miss Osmon."

The doctor wasted no time with his physical examination, then proceeded to ask her a series of questions—everything from the calendar date to what she'd had for breakfast. His unconcerned expression afterward told her she must have passed.

"I think you'll be just fine. Though quite sore for the next several weeks. You don't appear to be concussed. But someone will need to watch you for the next twenty-four hours or so. Just to be on the safe side." He motioned to the door. "Mind if I let your boyfriend in? He appears to be very concerned about you."

"Oh, he's not—they're just the—"

The doctor raised an eyebrow in question. "I apologize. He took care of the necessary paperwork and already settled the fees. I just assumed."

He had settled the bill? A nagging sense of discomfort blossomed in her chest. This stranger had paid for her care. She would have to figure out how to pay him back. Not that it would be easy.

The physician continued, "In any case, if he's

the one who'll be watching you, he'll need to hear this."

"He won't be watching me. I have a friend—"

Before she got the last word out, Greta came barreling through the door, her springy gray hair still wrapped tight in a kitchen hairnet.

"Yowza," the older woman exclaimed as soon as her gaze landed on Mel's face. "You look like you went a couple rounds with a prizefighter. Or were ya fighting over a discounted item at The Basement? Their shoppers can be brutal!"

"Hi, Greta. Thanks for coming."

"Sure thing, kid. I took a cab over as soon as we heard. You doin' okay?" She'd left the door wide-open behind her. The two strangers hovered uncertainly out in the hallway, both of them giving her concerned looks.

Mel sighed. *What the heck? May as well make this a standing room—only crowd.* After all, they were nice enough to bring her in and take care of the processing while she was being examined. She motioned for them to come in. The taller, more handsome one stepped inside first. His friend followed close behind.

"The doctor says I'll be fine," she told them.

The doctor nodded. "I also said she needs to be monitored overnight. To make sure there are no signs of concussion or other trauma." He addressed the room in general before turning to Mel directly. "If you feel nauseous or dizzy, or if over-the-counter medications don't seem to be addressing the pain, you need to come back in. Understood?"

"Yes."

He turned to the others. "You need to watch for any sign of blacking out or loss of balance."

Greta nodded. As did the two men for some reason.

The doctor gave a quick wave before hastily walking out.

Mel smiled awkwardly at the two men. It occurred to her she didn't even know their names. "Um… I'm Mel."

They exchanged a glance between them. Then the taller one stepped forward. "I'm Ray. This is Sal." He motioned to his friend, who politely nodded.

More awkwardness ensued as all four of them stood silent.

"I'm Greta," the older woman suddenly and very loudly offered.

Both men said hello. Finally, Greta reached for Mel's arm. "C'mon, kiddo. Let's get you dressed. Then we'll call for a cab so we can get you home."

Ray stepped forward. "That won't be necessary. We'll take you anywhere you need to go."

Ray sighed with relief for what must have been the hundredth time as the old lady directed them to the front of a small eatery not far from where the accident had occurred. Thank goodness that Mel appeared to be all right. But she was sporting one devil of a shiner on her right eye and the whole side of her face looked a purple mess.

For some inexplicable reason, his mind kept referring to the moment he'd picked her up and carried her to the car. The softness of her as he'd held her, the way she'd smelled. Some delicate scent of flowers combined with a fruity shampoo he'd noticed when her head had been under his nose.

"This is our stop," Greta declared and reached for the door handle.

Ray immediately got out of the car to assist Mel out onto the street. After all, the older woman looked barely able to get herself moving. She'd actually dozed off twice during the short ride over. Ray hadn't missed how Mel had positioned herself to allow Greta to lean against her shoulder as she snored softly. Despite her injury. Nor how she'd gently nudged her friend awake as they approached their destination.

Who was taking care of whom in this scenario?

How in the world was this frail, seemingly exhausted older lady supposed to keep an eye on her injured friend all night?

Ray would never forgive himself if Mel had any kind of medical disaster in the middle of the night. Despite his reassurances, the doctor had made it clear she wasn't completely out of the woods just yet.

"My sister and I live in a flat above this diner, which we own and manage," Greta informed him around a wide yawn as the three of them approached the door. She rummaged around in her oversize bag for several moments, only to come up empty.

"Dang it. I guess I left my keys behind when I rushed over to the hospital."

She reached for a panel by the side of the door and pressed a large button. A buzzer could be heard sounding upstairs. Several beats passed and…nothing.

Mel offered him a shy smile. Her black hair glistened like tinsel where the streetlight hit it. The neon light of the diner sign above them brought out the bright evergreen hue of her eyes. Well, the one that wasn't nearly swollen shut anyway. The poor woman probably couldn't wait to get upstairs and lie down.

Unfortunately, she would have to wait a bit longer. Several more moments passed. Greta pressed the button at least half a dozen more times. Ray wasn't any more reassured as they continued to wait.

Finally, after what seemed like an eternity, the sound of shuffling feet could be heard approaching as a shadow moved closer to the opposite side of the door. When it finally opened, they were greeted by a groggy, disheveled woman who was even older than Greta. She didn't even look fully awake yet.

It was settled. There was no way he could leave an injured woman with the likes of these two ladies. His conscience wouldn't allow it. Especially not when he was partly responsible for said injury to begin with.

"I'm glad that's over with." Saleh started the SUV as soon as Ray opened the passenger door and leaned into the vehicle. "Let's finally get to our hotel, then. I could use a long hot shower and a tall glass of something strong and aromatic." He reached for the gearshift before giving him a quizzical look. "Why aren't you getting in the car?"

"I've decided to stay here."

Saleh's eyes went wide with shock. "What?"

"I can't leave the young lady, Saleh. You should see the older sister who's supposed to watch Mel with Greta."

"You mean Greta's the younger one?"

"Believe it or not."

"Still. It's no longer our concern. We've done

all we can. She'll be fine." He motioned with a tilt of his head for Rayhan to get in the car.

"I'm going to stay here and make sure of it. You go on ahead and check us into the hotel."

"You can't be serious. Are you forgetting who you are?"

Ray bit down on his impatience. Saleh was a trusted friend. But right now, he was the one close to forgetting who he was and whom he was addressing.

"Not in the least. I happen to be part of the reason that young lady is up there, sporting all sorts of cuts and bruises, as well as a potential head injury, which needs to be monitored. By someone who can actually keep an eye on her with some degree of competence."

"Your Highness, I understand all that. But staying here is not wise."

"Don't call me that, Saleh. You know better."

"I'm just trying to remind you of your position. Perhaps I should also remind you that this isn't an announced state visit. If these ladies were to find out who you are, it could leak to the rest of the world before morning. The resulting frenzy of press could easily result in an embarrassing media nightmare for the monarchy. Not to mention Verdovia as a whole."

"They won't find out."

Saleh huffed in exasperation. "How can you be sure?"

Ray ignored the question as he didn't really have any kind of adequate answer. "I've made up my mind," he said with finality.

"There's more to it. Isn't there, Rayhan?"

Ray knew exactly what his friend meant. The two had known each other their whole lives, since they were toddlers kicking around a sponge soccer ball in the royal courtyard. He wouldn't bother to deny what his friend had clearly observed.

"I saw the way you were looking at her," Saleh threw out as if issuing a challenge. "With much more than sympathy in your eyes. Admit it. There's more to it."

Ray only sighed. "Perhaps there is, my friend." He softly shut the car door.

Ray was asleep on Frannie and Greta's couch. Mel popped two anti-inflammatory pills into her mouth and then took a swig of water to swallow them down. Her borrowed nightgown felt snug against her hips. It belonged to Greta, who could accurately be described as having the figure of a very thin teenage boy. A description that didn't fit Mel in any way.

The feel of her nightwear wouldn't be the only thing bothering her tonight, Mel figured. The man lying in the other room only a few feet away would no doubt disrupt her sleep. Had she ever felt so aware of a man before? She honestly couldn't say, despite having been married. He had such a magnetism, she'd be hard-pressed to put its impact on her into words. Everything about him screamed class and breeding. From the impeccable and, no doubt, expensive tailored clothing to the SUV he and his friend were driving around in, Ray was clearly not lacking in resources. He was well-mannered and well-spoken. And judging by what he'd done earlier tonight, he was quite kindhearted.

Ray had feigned being too tired to travel with his friend to their hotel across town and had asked the Perlman sisters if he could crash on their couch instead. Mel wasn't buying it in the least. First of all, he didn't seem the type of man to lack stamina in any way. No, his true intention was painfully obvious. He'd taken one look at Frannie, studied Greta again and then perused Mel's battered face and decided he couldn't leave her in the care of the elderly sisters. None of them questioned it. Sure, Ray was barely more than a stranger, but he'd had ample opportunity if his motives were at all nefarious.

Besides, he hardly appeared to be a kidnapper. And he definitely wasn't likely to be a thief looking to take off with the Perlman sisters' ancient and cracked bone china.

No, he was just a gentleman who'd not only made sure to take care of her after she'd got hurt, he'd insisted on hanging around to keep an eye on her.

She crawled into the twin bed the Perlman sisters kept set up in their spare room and eyed the functional sleigh-bell ornament taken off the diner Christmas tree that Greta had handed her before going to bed. She was supposed to ring it to arouse their attention if she felt at all ill during the night. As if either sister had any chance of hearing it. Frannie hadn't even heard the much louder door buzzer earlier this evening. No wonder Ray had insisted on staying.

She felt oddly touched by his thoughtfulness. Not every man would have been so concerned.

She tried to imagine Eric going out of his way in such a fashion under similar circumstances. Simply to help a stranger. She couldn't picture it. No, Ray didn't seem at all like her ex. In fact, he was unlike any other man she'd ever met. And his looks! The man was heart-stoppingly handsome. She still didn't know where he was from, but based on his dark coloring and regal features, she would guess somewhere in the Mediterranean. Southern Italy perhaps. Maybe Greece. Or even somewhere in the Middle East.

Mel sighed again and snuggled deeper into her pillow. What did any of her speculation matter in the overall scheme of things? Men like Ray weren't the type a divorced waitress could count among her acquaintances. He would be nothing more than a flash of brightness that passed through her life for a brief moment in time. By this time next week, no doubt, he wouldn't give the likes of Melinda Osmon more than a lingering thought.

* * *

"So did she even find a dress?"

"I guess so. She says she lost the shopping bag 'cause of the accident, though."

"So no dress. I guess she definitely isn't going to the ball, then."

"Nope. Not without a dress. And not with that crazy shiner where her eye is."

What was it about this dress everyone kept talking about? Ray stirred and slowly opened his eyes. To his surprise it was morning already. He'd slept surprisingly well on the lumpy velvet-covered couch the sisters had offered him last night. Said sisters were currently talking much too loudly in the kitchen, which was off to the side of the apartment. Clearly, they didn't entertain overnight guests often.

His thoughts immediately shifted to Mel. How was she feeling? He'd slept more soundly than he'd expected to. What if she'd needed something in the middle of the night? He swiftly strode to the kitchen. "Has anyone checked on Mel yet?"

Both ladies halted midspeech to give him curious looks. "Well, good morning to you, too," Greta said with just a touch of grouchiness in her voice. Or maybe that was Frannie. In matching terry robes and thick glasses perched on the ends of their noses, they looked remarkably similar.

"I apologize. I just wondered about our patient."

The two women raised their eyebrows at him. "She's *our* patient now, huh?" one of the women asked.

Luckily, the other one spoke before Ray could summon an answer to that question. "She's sleeping soundly. I sneaked a peek at her as soon as I woke up. Breathing nice and even. Even has some color back in her face. Well, real color. Aside from the nasty purple bruise."

Ray felt the tension he wasn't aware he held slowly leave his chest and shoulders. One of the women pulled a chair out for him as another handed him a steaming cup of coffee. Both actions were done with a no-nonsense efficiency. Ray gratefully took the steaming cup and sat down.

The small flat was a far cry from the majestic expanse of the castle he called home, but the sheer homeliness and coziness of the setting served to put him in a comfortable state of ease, one that took him a bit by surprise. He spent most of his life in a harried state of rushing from one activity or responsibility to another. To be able to simply sit and enjoy a cup of coffee in a quaint New England kitchen was a novel experience. One he was enjoying more than he would have guessed.

"Damn shame about the dress," Greta or Frannie commented as she sat down across him, the other lady joining them a moment later after refreshing her mug. He really needed one of them to somehow identify herself or he was bound to make an embarrassing slip before the morning was over about who was who.

"Can someone tell me what the deal is with this dress?" he asked.

"Mel was coming back from shopping when you and your friend knocked her on her keister," the sister right next to him answered.

"Frannie!" the other one exclaimed. Thank goodness. Now he just had to keep straight which was which once they stood. "That's no way to talk to our guest," she added.

Ray took a sip of his coffee, the guilt washing over him once more. Though technically they hadn't been the ones to actually run into Mel—the cyclist had done that—he couldn't help but feel that if Saleh had been paying better attention, Mel wouldn't be in the state she was in currently.

"She lost the shopping bag in all the confusion," Frannie supplied.

"I'm terribly sorry to hear that," Ray answered. "It must have been some dress. I'll have to find a way to compensate for Mel's losing it."

"It's more what she needed it for."

Ray found himself oddly curious. When was the last time he cared about why a woman needed an article of clothing? Never. The answer to that question was a resounding *never*.

"What did she need it for?"

"To stick it to that scoundrel husband of hers."

Ray found himself on the verge of sputtering out the coffee he'd just taken a sip of. Husband. Mel was married. It really wasn't any of his business. So why did he feel like someone had just landed a punch in the middle of his gut? He'd met the woman less than twelve hours ago for heaven's sake. Had barely spoken more than a few words to her.

"He's her ex-husband," Greta clarified. "But my sister's right about the scoundrel part."

"Oh?" Ray inquired. For the second time already this morning, he felt like a solid weight had been lifted off his shoulders. So she wasn't actually married currently. He cursed internally as he thought it. What bit of difference did it make where he was concerned?

"Yeah, he took all her money, then left her for some flirty flirt of a girl who works for him."

That did sound quite scoundrel-like. A pang of sympathy blossomed in his chest. No woman deserved that. What little he knew of Mel, she seemed like she wouldn't hurt another being if her life depended on it. She certainly didn't deserve such treatment.

"Before they got divorced, Mel and her ex were always invited to the mayor's annual charity holiday ball. The mayor's daughter is a college friend of both of theirs. This year that no-good ex of Mel's is taking his new lady.

Word is, he proposed to her and they'll be attending as doctor and fiancée."

Frannie nodded as her sister spoke. "Yeah, we were trying to convince her to go anyway. 'Cause why should he have the satisfaction? But she had nothing to wear. We gave her an advance on her paycheck and told her to find the nicest dress she could afford."

Ray sat silent, taking all this in. Several points piqued his interest, not the least of which being just how much these ladies seemed to care for the young lady who worked for them. Mel was clearly more than a mere employee. She was family and so they were beyond outraged on her behalf.

The other thing was that she'd been trying to tell him right there on the sidewalk about how important the dress was, and he hadn't bothered to listen. He had just assumed that she'd hit her head and didn't know what she was talking about. He felt guilt wash over him anew.

"I still wish there was a way she could go." Greta shook her head with regret. "That awful man needs to know she don't give a damn about him and that she's still going to attend these events. With or without him."

A heavy silence settled over the room before Frannie broke it with a clap of her hands. "You know, I got a great idea," she declared to her sister with no small display of excitement.

"What's that?"

"I know she don't have anything to wear, but if she can figure that out, I think Ray here should take her." She flashed a brilliant smile in his direction.

Greta gasped in agreement, nodding vehemently. "Ooh, excellent idea. Why, he'd make for the perfect date!"

Frannie turned to him, a mischievous sparkle in her eyes. "It's the least you can do. You did knock her on her keister."

Greta nodded solemnly next to him.

This unexpected turn proved to take him off guard. Ray tried to muster what exactly to say. He was spared the effort.

Mel chose that moment to step into the room. It was clear she'd heard the bulk of the conversation. She looked far from pleased.

* * *

Mel pulled out a chair and tried to clamp down on her horror. She could hardly believe what she'd heard. As much as she loved the Perlman sisters, sometimes they went just a tad too far. In this case, they'd traveled miles. The last thing she wanted from any man, let alone a man the likes of Ray, was some kind of sympathy date. And she'd be sure to tell both the ladies that as soon as she got them alone.

For now, she had to try to hide her mortification from their overnight guest.

"How do you feel, dear?" Greta asked.

"Fine. Just fine."

"The swelling seems to be going down," Frannie supplied.

Mel merely nodded. She risked a glance at Ray from the corner of her eye. To his credit, he looked equally uncomfortable.

Frannie stood suddenly. "Well, the two of us should get downstairs and start prepping for the weekend diner crowd." She rubbed Mel's shoulder. "There's still fresh coffee in the pot. You obviously have the day off."

Mel started to argue, but Frannie held up a

hand to stop her. Greta piped up from across the table. "Don't even think about it. You rest and concentrate on healing. We can handle the diner today."

Mel nodded reluctantly as the two sisters left the kitchen to go get ready for their morning. It was hard to stay aggravated with those two.

Except now she was alone with Ray. The awkwardness hung like thick, dense fog in the air. If she was smart, she would have walked away and pretended not to hear anything that was said.

Of all the...

What would possess Greta and Frannie to suggest such a thing? She couldn't imagine what Ray must be feeling. They had put him in such a sufferable position.

To her surprise, he broke the silence with an apology. "I'm so terribly sorry, Mel."

Great, he was apologizing for not taking her up on the sisters' offer. Well, that got her hackles up. She wasn't the one who had asked him to take her to the ball.

"There's no need to apologize," she said, perhaps a little too curtly. "I really had no intention of attending that party anyway. I hardly need a date for an event I'm not going to. Not that I would have necessarily said yes." Now, why had she felt compelled to add that last bit?

Ray's jaw fell open. "Oh, I meant. I just—I should have listened when you were trying to tell me about your dress. I didn't realize you'd dropped your parcel."

Mel suddenly realized her mistake. He was simply offering a general apology. He wasn't even referring to the ball. She felt the color drain from her face from the embarrassment. If she could, she would have sunk through the floor and into another dimension. Never to be seen or heard from again. Talk about flattering oneself.

She cleared her throat, eager to change the subject. Although this next conversation was going to be only slightly less cringeworthy. "I was going to mention this last night, but you ended up staying the night."

"Yes?"

"I know you paid for my hospital visit. I have every intention of paying you back." Here was the tough part. "I, um, will just need to mail it to you. It's a bit hard to reimburse you right at this moment."

He immediately shook his head. "You don't need to worry about that."

"I insist. Please just let me know where I can mail a check as soon as I get a chance."

"I won't accept it, Mel."

She crossed her arms in front of her chest. "You don't understand. It's important to me that I pay back my debts." Unlike her ex-husband, she added silently.

He actually waved his hand in dismissal. "There really is no need."

No need? What part about her feeling uncomfortable about being indebted to him was he unable to comprehend? His next words gave her a clue.

"Given your circumstances, I don't want you to feel you owe me anything."

Mel felt the surge of ire prickle over her skin. She should have known. His meaning couldn't be clearer. Ray was no different than all the other wealthy people she'd known. Exactly like the ones who'd made her parents' lives so miserable.

"My circumstances? I certainly don't need your charity, if that's what you mean."

His eyes grew wide. "Of course not. I apologize. I meant no offense. I'm fluent, but English is my second language, after all. I simply meant that I feel responsible for you incurring the fees in the first place."

"But you weren't responsible. The cyclist was. And he's clearly not available, so the responsibility of my hospital bill is mine and mine alone."

He studied her through narrowed eyes. "Is it that important to you?"

"It is."

He gave her a slight nod of acquiescence. "Then I shall make sure to give you my contact information before I leave so that you can forward reimbursement at your convenience."

"Thank you."

Ray cleared his throat before continuing, "Also, if you'll allow me, I'd love to attend the Boston mayor's annual holiday ball as your escort."

CHAPTER THREE

MEL BLINKED AND gave her head a small shake, the action sending a pounding ache through her cheek straight up to her eye. In her shock, she'd forgotten how sore she was. But Ray had indeed just shocked her. Or maybe she hadn't actually heard him correctly. Maybe she really did have a serious head injury that was making her imagine things.

"I'm sorry. What did you just say?"

His lips curved into a small smile and Mel felt a knot tighten in the depths of her core. The man was sinfully handsome when he smiled. "I said I'd like to attend the ball with you."

She gently placed her coffee cup on the table in front of her. Oh, for heaven's sake. She couldn't wait to give Frannie and Greta a speaking-to. "You don't need to do that, Ray. You also didn't need to cover my expenses. And you didn't need to stay last night. You've done more than enough already. Is this because I insist on repaying you?" she asked. How much of a charity case did he think she was? Mel felt her anger rising once more.

But he shook his head. "Has nothing to do with that."

"The accident wasn't even your fault."

"This has nothing to do with the accident either."

"Of course it does. And I'm trying to tell you, you don't need to feel that you have to make anything up to me. Again, the accident yesterday was not your fault."

He leaned closer to her over the table. "But you don't understand. It would actually be something of a quid pro quo to take me to this ball. You'd actually be the one doing me a favor."

Okay, that settled it. She knew she was hearing things. In fact, she was probably still back in Frannie and Greta's guest room, soundly asleep. This was all a strange dream. Or maybe she'd accidentally taken too many painkillers. There was no way this could actually be happening. There was absolutely nothing someone like Mel could offer a man such as Ray. The idea that accompanying her to the ball would be a favor to *him* was ridiculous.

"Come again?"

"Allow me to explain," Ray continued at her confused look. "I'm here on business on behalf of the king of Verdovia. He is looking to acquire some property in the Boston area. The type of people attending an event that the mayor is throwing are precisely the type of people I'd like to have direct contact with."

"So you're saying you actually want to go? To meet local business people?"

He nodded. "Precisely. And in the process, we can do the two-birds-killing."

She was beginning to suspect they both had some kind of brain trauma. Then his meaning dawned on her. He was misstating the typical American idiom.

"You mean kill two birds with one stone?"

He smiled again, wider this time, causing Mel's toes to curl in her slippers. "Correct. Though I never did understand that expression. Who wants to kill even one bird, let alone two?"

She had to agree.

"In any case, you help me meet some of these local business people, and I'll make sure you stick your ex-husband."

She couldn't help it. She had to laugh. This was all so surreal. It was like she was in a completely different reality than the one she'd woken up in yesterday morning. "You mean stick it to."

"That's right," he replied, responding to her laugh with one of his own.

For just a split second, she was tempted to say yes, that she'd do it. But then the ridiculousness of the whole idea made her pause. It was such a harebrained scheme. No one would believe Mel and someone like Ray were an actual couple. An unbidden image of the two of them dancing close, chest to chest, flashed in her mind. A curl of heat moved through the pit of her stomach before she squelched it. What a silly fantasy.

They clearly had nothing in common. Not that she would know with any real certainty, of course. She didn't know the man at all.

"What do you think?" Ray prompted.

"I think there's no way it would work. For

one thing, we've barely met. You don't know a thing about me and I don't know a thing about you. I have no idea who you are. How would we even begin to explain why we're at such an event together?"

A sly twinkle appeared in his eye. "That's easy to fix. We should spend some time getting to know each other. Can I interest you in breakfast? I understand there's an excellent eating establishment very nearby. Right downstairs, as a matter of fact."

Greta seated them in a corner booth and handed him a large laminated menu. The giant smile on the older woman's face gave every bit the impression that she was beyond pleased at seeing the two of them at breakfast together. Though she did initially appear quite surprised.

Well, Ray had also surprised himself this morning. He'd had no idea that he'd intended to ask to take her to the mayor's ball until the words were actually leaving his mouth. Saleh would want to throttle him for such a foolish move. Oh, well, he'd worry about Saleh later. Ray's reasons were sound if one really thought about it. So he'd exaggerated his need to meet local business leaders, considering he already had the contacts in Boston that he needed. But Mel didn't know that or need to know that. And what harm would it do? What was so wrong about wanting to take her to the ball and hoping she'd have a good time there? Between the terrible accident yesterday and what he'd found out this morning about her past history, she could definitely use some fun, he figured. Even if it was only for a few hours.

Why he wanted to be the one to give that to her, he couldn't quite explain. He found himself wishing he'd met her under different circumstances, at a different time.

Right. He would have to be a completely different person for it to make an iota of difference. The reality was that he was the crown prince of Verdovia. He'd been groomed since birth to be beholden to rules and customs and to do what was best for the kingdom. He couldn't forget this trip was simply a temporary respite from all that.

This ball would give him a chance to do something different, out of the norm, if he attended as an associate of the royal family rather than as the prince. After all, wasn't that why he was in the United Sates? For one final adventure. This was a chance to attend a grand gala without all the pressures of being the Verdovian prince and heir to the throne.

He asked Mel to order for them both and she did so before Greta poured them some more coffee and then left their booth, her smile growing wider by the second.

"All right," Mel began once they were alone. "Tell me about yourself. Why don't you start with more about what you do for a living?"

Ray knew he had to tread carefully. He didn't want to lie to her, but he had to be careful to guard his true identity. Not only for his sake, but for hers, as well.

"You said something about acquiring real estate for the Verdovian royal family. Does that mean real estate is your main focus?" she asked.

Ray took a sip of his steamy beverage. He'd never had so much coffee in one sitting, but the Boston brew was strong and satisfying. "So to speak. I'm responsible for various duties in service of the king. He'd like to expand his American property holdings, particularly in metropolitan cities. He's been eyeing various high-end hotels in the Boston area. I volunteered to fly down here to scope out some prospects and perhaps make an agreement." Technically, he was telling her the complete truth.

Mel nodded. "I see. You're definitely a heavy hitter."

That wasn't an expression that made immediate sense to him. "You think I hit heavy?"

"Never mind. Do you have a family?"

"My parents and two younger sisters."

"What would you tell me about them?"

This part could get tricky if he wasn't careful. He hated being on the slim side of deceitful but what choice did he have? And in the overall scheme of things, what did it hurt that Mel didn't know he was a prince? In fact, he'd be glad to be able to forget the fact himself for just a brief moment in time.

"My father is a very busy man. Responsible for many people and lots of land. My mother is an accomplished musician who has studied the violin under some of Europe's masters and composes her own pieces."

Mel let out a low whistle. "Wow. That's quite a pedigree," she said in a near whisper. "How'd you end up picking such a high-profile career?"

He had to tread carefully answering that one. "It was chosen for me," he answered truthfully.

She lifted an eyebrow. "You mean the king chose you?"

He nodded. Again, it was the complete truth. "There were certain expectations made of me, being the only son of the family."

"Expectations?"

"Yes. It was a given that I would study business, that I would work in a career that led to the further wealth and prosperity of our island kingdom. Otherwise..."

The turn in conversation was throwing him off. Mel's questions brought up memories he hadn't given any consideration to in years.

She leaned farther toward him, over the table. "Otherwise what?"

He sighed, trying hard to clamp down on the years-old resentments that were suddenly re-surfacing in a most unwelcome way. Mel stared at him with genuine curiosity shining in her eyes. He'd never discussed this aspect of his life with anyone before. Not really. No one had bothered to ask, because it was all such a moot point.

"Otherwise, it wasn't a career I would have chosen for myself. I was a bit of an athlete. Played striker during school and university. Got several recruitment offers from coaches at major football clubs. Though you would call it soccer here."

She blinked. "So wait. You turned down the opportunity of a lifetime because the king had other plans?"

Ray tapped the tip of his finger against the tabletop. "That about sums it up, yes."

She blew out a breath. "Wow. That's loyalty."

"Well, loyalty happens to be a quality that was hammered into me since birth."

"What about your sisters?" she asked him. "Are they held to such high standards, as well?"

Ray shook his head. "No. Being younger, they have the luxury of much fewer demands being made of them."

"Lucky for them. What are they like?"

"Well, both are quite trying. Completely un-bearable brats," he told her. But he was unable to keep the tender smile off his face and his affection for his siblings out of his voice despite his words.

That earned him a small smile. "I'm guessing they're quite fortunate in having you as a brother." She sighed. "I don't have any siblings. I grew up an only child." Her tone suggested she was somewhat sad about the fact.

"That can have its advantages," he said, thinking of Saleh and the rather indulgent way the man's family treated him. "What of your parents?"

Mel looked away toward the small jukebox on the table, but not before he caught the small quiver in her chin. "I lost them about three years ago. They passed within months of each other."

"I'm so terribly sorry."

"Thank you for saying that."

"To lose them so close together must have been so difficult."

He couldn't help but reach for her hand across the table to comfort her. To his surprise and pleasure, she gripped his fingers, taking what he offered her.

"It was. My father got sick. There was nothing that could be done. It crushed my mom. She suffered a fatal cardiac event not long after." She let go of his fingers to brush away a tiny speck of a tear from the corner of her eye. "It was as if she couldn't go on without him. Her heart literally broke. They'd been together since they were teens."

Ray couldn't help but feel touched. To think of two people who had decided at such a young age that they cared for each other and stayed together throughout all those years. His own parents loved each other deeply, he knew. But their relationship had started out so ceremonial and preplanned. The same way his own marriage would begin.

The king and queen had worked hard to cultivate their affection into true love. He could only hope for as much for himself when the time came.

A realization dawned on him. Mel had been betrayed by the man she'd married within a couple of years of losing her parents. It was a wonder the woman could even smile or laugh.

He cleared his throat, trying to find a way to ask about her husband. But she was way ahead of him.

"You should probably know a little about my marriage."

"Aside from the knowledge that Frannie and Greta refer to him as 'that scoundrel,' you mean?"

This time the smile didn't quite reach her eyes. "I guess that would be one way to describe him."

"What happened?" He knew the man had left his wife for another woman. Somehow he'd also left Mel to fend for herself without much in the way of finances. He waited as Mel filled in some of the holes in the story.

She began slowly, softly, the hurt in her voice as clear as a Verdovian sunrise. "We met at school. At homecoming, our first year there. He was the most attentive and loving boyfriend. Very ambitious, knew from the beginning that he wanted to be a dentist. Husband material, you would think."

Ray simply waited as she spoke, not risking an interruption.

"When I lost my parents, I couldn't bear to live in their house. So I put it on the market. He invited me to live with him in his small apartment while he attended dental school. Eventually, he asked me to marry him. I'd just lost my whole family…"

She let the words trail off, but he could guess how the sentence might end. Mel had found herself suddenly alone, reeling from the pain of loss. A marriage proposal from the man she'd been seeing all through college had probably seemed like a gift.

"My folks' house netted a good amount in the sale. Plus they'd left me a modest yet impressive nest egg."

She drew in a shaky breath.

"Here's the part where I demonstrate my foolishness. Eric and I agreed that we would spend the money on his dentistry schooling after college graduation. That way we could start our lives together free of any school loans when he finished. I handed over all my savings and worked odd jobs here and there to cover any other costs while he attended classes and studied. When he was through, it was supposed to be my turn to continue on to a higher degree. I studied art history in my undergrad. Not a huge job market for those majors." She used one hand to motion around the restaurant. "Hence the waitressing gig. At the time, though, I was set on pursuing a teaching degree and maybe working as an elementary school art teacher. Once we had both achieved our dreams, I thought we would start a family." She said the last words on a wistful sigh.

Ray didn't need to hear the rest. What a foolish man her former husband was. Mel was quite a beautiful woman, even with the terrible degree of bruising on her face. Her injuries couldn't hide her strong, angular features, nor did they diminish the sparkling brightness of her jewel-green eyes.

From what he could tell, she was beautiful on the inside, too. She'd given herself fully to the man she'd made marriage vows to—albeit with some naïveté—to the point of generously granting him all the money she had. Only to be paid back with pure betrayal. Her friends obviously thought the world of her. To boot, she was a witty and engaging conversationalist. In fact, he wouldn't even be able to tell how long they'd been sitting in this booth, as time seemed to have stood still while they spoke.

"Frannie and Greta are sorely accurate in their description of this Eric, then. He must be a scoundrel and a complete fool to walk away from you."

Mel ducked her head shyly at the compliment, then tucked a strand of hair behind her ear. When she spoke again, she summoned a stronger tone. He hoped it was because his words had helped to bolster some of her confidence, even if only a little.

"I have to take some of the blame. I moved too quickly, was too anxious to be a member of a family again."

"I think you're being too hard on yourself."

"Enough of the sad details," she said. "Let's talk about other things."

"Such as?"

"What are your interests? Do you have any hobbies? What type of music do you like?"

She was trying valiantly to change the subject. He went along.

For the next several minutes, they talked about everything from each other's favorite music to the type of cuisine they each preferred. Even after their food arrived, the conversation remained fluid and constant. It made no sense, given the short amount of time spent in each other's company, but Ray was beginning to feel as if he knew the young lady across him better than most of the people in his regular orbit.

And he was impressed. Something about her pulled to him unlike anyone else he'd ever encountered. She had a pure authentic quality that he'd been hard-pressed to find throughout his lifetime. Most people didn't act like themselves around the crown prince of Verdovia. Ray could count on one hand all the people in his life he felt he truly knew deep down.

As he thought of Saleh, Ray's phone went off again in his pocket. That had to be at least the tenth time. If Mel was aware of the incessant buzzing of his phone, she didn't let on. And Ray didn't bother to reply to Saleh's repeated calls. He'd already left a voice message for him this morning, letting his friend know that he'd be further delayed.

Besides, he was enjoying Mel's company too much to break away simply for Saleh's sake. The other man could wait.

"So just to be sure we make this official." He extended his hand out to her after an extended lull in their lively conversation. "May I please have the pleasure of accompanying you to the mayor's annual holiday ball?"

She let out a small laugh. "You know what? Why not?"

Ray held a hand to his chest in mock offense. "Well, that's certainly the least enthusiastic acceptance I've received from a lady. But I'll take it."

It surprised him how much he was looking forward to it. Even so, a twinge of guilt nagged at him for his duplicity. He'd give anything to completely come clean to Mel about who he was and what he was doing here in the city. Something shifted in his chest at the possibility of her finding out the truth and being disappointed in him. But he had no choice. He'd been groomed to do what was best for Verdovia and its people.

As Mel had phrased it earlier, though, the king had other plans for him.

CHAPTER FOUR

A LIGHT DUSTING of snow sprinkled the scenery outside the window by their table. Mel couldn't remember the last time she'd had such a lighthearted and fun conversation. Despite his classy demeanor, Ray had a way of putting her at ease. Plus, he seemed genuinely interested in what she had to say. He had to be a busy man, yet here he still sat as the morning grew later, happy to simply chat with her.

She motioned to Ray's plate. She'd been a little apprehensive ordering for him. He didn't strike her as the type who was used to diner cuisine. But he'd done a pretty nice job of clearing his plate. He must have liked it a little. "So, what did you think? I know baked beans first thing in the morning is an acquired taste. It's a Boston thing."

"Hence the name 'Boston Baked Beans'?"

"Correct."

"I definitely feel full. Not exactly a light meal."

She felt a flutter of disappointment in her stomach. Of course, she'd ordered the wrong thing. What did she know about what an international businessman would want for breakfast? She was completely out of her element around this man. And here she'd just agreed to attend a grand charity gala with him. Pretending she was his date. As if she could pull off such a thing.

"But it definitely—how do you Americans say it?—landed in the spot."

His mistake on the expression, along with a keen sense of relief, prompted a laugh out of her. "Hit the spot," she corrected.

"Yes, that's it. It definitely hit the spot."

His phone vibrated for the umpteenth time in his pocket. He'd been so good about not checking it, she was starting to feel guilty. He was here on a business trip, after all.

She also hadn't missed the lingering looks he'd received from all the female diner patrons, young and old alike. From the elderly ladies heading to their daily hair appointments to the young co-eds who attended the city's main university, located a shuttle ride away.

"I know you must have a lot to do. I probably shouldn't keep you much longer."

Ray sighed with clear resignation. "Unfortunately, there are some matters I should attend to." He started to reach for his pocket. "What do I owe for the breakfast?"

She held up a hand to stop him. "Please, employee privilege. It's on me."

"Are you sure? It's not going to come out of your wages or anything, is it?"

Not this again. It wasn't like she was a pauper. Just that she was trying to put some money away in order to finally get the advanced degree she'd always intended to study for. Before fate in the form of Eric Fuller had yanked that dream away from her.

"It so happens, Greta and Frannie consider free meals part of my employee package." Though she normally wouldn't have ordered this much food for herself over the course of a full week, let alone in one sitting. Something told her the two ladies didn't mind. Not judging by the immensely pleased smirks they kept sending in her direction when Ray wasn't looking.

"Well, thank you. I can't recall the last time I was treated to a meal by such a beautiful woman."

Whoa. This man was the very definition of *charming*. She had no doubt that had to be one doozy of a fib. Beautiful women probably cooked for him all the time.

"But you're right, I should probably be going."

She nodded and started to pile the empty plates in the center of the table. Waitress habit.

"Can I walk you back upstairs?" Ray asked.

She wanted to decline. Lord knew he'd spent enough time with her already. But a very vocal part of her didn't want this morning to end. "I'd like that," she found herself admitting.

He stood and offered her his arm. She gently put her hand in the crook of his elbow after he helped her out of the booth. With a small wave of thanks to her two bosses, they proceeded toward the side door, which led to the stairway to the apartment.

"So I'll call you tomorrow, then?" Ray asked. "To discuss further details for Saturday night?"

"That sounds good. And I'll work on finding a plan B for what my attire will be."

His mouth furrowed into a frown, causing deep lines to crease his forehead. "I'd forgotten about that. Again, I'm so terribly sorry for not paying more attention as you were telling me about your parcel."

She let out a small laugh. "It's okay. It wasn't exactly a situation conducive to listening."

"Still, I feel like a cad."

"It's all right," she reassured him. "I'm sure Frannie and Greta won't mind if I do some rummaging in their closet. They might have something bordering on suitable."

He paused on the foot of the stairs right as she took the first step up. The difference in height brought them eye to eye, close enough that the scent of him tickled her nose, a woodsy, spicy scent as unique as he was.

"I'm afraid that won't do at all." His eyes looked genuinely troubled.

"It's all right. I'm very creative. And I'm a whiz with a sewing machine."

"That may be, but even creative geniuses need the necessary tools. Not to mention time. Something tells me you're not going to find anything appropriate in any closet up in that apartment." He pointed to the ceiling.

It wasn't like she had much choice. She'd already spent what little she could afford on the now-missing dress. All her closest friends had moved out of the New England area, so it wasn't as if she could borrow something. She was out of options. A jarring thought struck her. Could this be Ray's subtle way of trying to back out of taking her? But that made no sense. He was the one who had insisted on going in the first place. Could he have had a sudden change of heart?

"There's only one thing to do. I believe I owe you one formal ball gown, Miss Osmon. Are you up for some shopping? Perhaps tomorrow?"

Mel immediately shook her head. She absolutely could not accept such an offer. "I can't allow you to do that, Ray. Thank you, but no."

"Why not?"

She would think it was obvious. She couldn't

allow herself to be this man's charity case. He'd done enough when he'd paid for her hospital bill, for goodness' sake. A sum she still had to figure out how to pay back. Further indebting herself to Ray was absolutely out of the question. She opened her mouth to tell him so.

He cut her off before she could begin. "What if I said it was more for me?"

A sharp gasp tore out of her throat. He had to be joking. That notion was so ridiculous, she actually bit back a laugh. He didn't look like the type, but what did she know? Looks could be deceiving. And she certainly wasn't one to judge.

He responded with a bark of laughter. "I see I've given you the wrong impression. I meant it would be for me in that if I'm trying to make an impression at this event with various people, I would prefer to have my date dressed for the occasion."

That certainly made sense, but still, essentially he would be buying her a dress. She cleared her throat, tried to focus on saying the right words without sounding offended. He really couldn't be faulted for the way he viewed the world. Not with all the material privilege he'd been afforded. She understood that better now after the conversation they'd just had together. Lord, it was hard to concentrate when those deep dark eyes were staring at her so close and so intently.

"If it makes you feel better, the gown can become the property of the royal family eventually. The queen is always looking for donated items to be auctioned off for various charities. I'll have it shipped straight to her afterward. I can pretend I was considerate enough to purchase it for that very purpose."

That cracked her resolve somewhat. Essentially, she'd only be borrowing a dress from him. Or more accurately, from the royal family of Verdovia. That was a bit more palatable, she supposed. Especially if in the end it would result in a charitable donation to a worthy cause.

Or maybe she was merely falling for his easy charm and finding ways to justify all that Ray was saying. Simply because she just couldn't think straight, given the way he was looking at her.

* * *

Saleh was already outside, idling on the curb in the SUV by the time Ray reluctantly left the diner. His friend did not look happy.

Ray opened the passenger door only to be greeted by a sigh of exasperation. No, definitely not happy in the least.

"After yesterday, maybe I should drive," Ray said before entering the car, just to further agitate him.

It worked. "You have not been answering your phone," Saleh said through gritted teeth.

"I was busy. The ladies treated me to an authentic New England breakfast. You should try it."

Saleh pulled into the street. "If only I hadn't already eaten a gourmet meal of warm scones made from scratch and fresh fruit accompanied by freshly squeezed orange juice at my five-star hotel."

Ray shrugged. "To each his own. I'm happy I got to try something a little different." Who would have thought that there were parts of the world where people had baked beans for breakfast?

"Is breakfast the only thing you tried?" Saleh removed his hands from the steering wheel long enough to place air quotes on the last word.

"What you're alluding to is preposterous, my friend. I simply wanted to make sure the young lady was all right after the accident. Nothing more."

Saleh seemed satisfied with that answer. "Great. Now that you've made sure, can we move on and forget all this unpleasantness of the accident?"

Ray shifted in his seat. "Well, not exactly."

Saleh's hands gripped the steering wheel so tightly, his knuckles whitened. "What exactly does 'not exactly' mean, my prince?"

"It means I may have made a commitment or two to Miss Osmon."

"Define these commitments, please."

"I'll be taking her shopping at some point."

"Shopping?"

"Yes. And, also, I'll be accompanying her to the Boston mayor's holiday charity ball on Saturday."

Saleh actually hit the brake, eliciting a loud

honk from several cars behind them. "You will do what?"

"Perhaps I should indeed drive," Ray teased.

Saleh took a breath and then regained the appropriate speed. "If you don't mind my asking, what the hell has got into you?"

"I'm simply trying to enjoy Christmastime in Boston."

"There are countless ways you can do that, Prince Rayhan. Ways that don't involve risking embarrassment to Verdovia and the monarchy behind it."

"I've already committed. I fully intend to go."

"But why?" the other man asked, clearly at a loss. "Why would you ever risk your identity being discovered?"

Ray pinched the bridge of his nose. He didn't want to have to explain himself, not about this. The truth was he wasn't sure even how to explain it. "I'll be careful to avoid that, Saleh. I've decided the risk is worth it." Mel was worth it.

"I don't understand. Not even a little."

Ray sighed, searched for the perfect words. If he couldn't confide in Saleh, there really was no one else on this earth he could confide in.

He had to try. "I'm not sure how to put it into words, Saleh. I felt something when I lifted her into my arms after she was hurt. The way she clung to me, shivering in my embrace. And since this morning, the more time I've spent with her, the more I want to. You must understand that. You must have felt that way before."

Saleh bit the inside of his cheek. "My wife and I were seven when we met."

Okay. Maybe Saleh wasn't the person who would understand. But he had to see where Ray was coming from.

"I just don't understand how this all came about. How in the world did you end up agreeing to attend a charity ball of all things? You always complain about having to frequent such affairs back home."

"It's a long story."

"We have a bit of a drive still."

Ray tried to summon the words that would make his friend understand. "It's different back home. There I'm the crown prince. Everyone who approaches me has some ulterior motive." Most especially the ladies, be it a photo opportunity or something more involved. "Or there's some pressing financial or property matter." Ray halted midspiel. He was bordering on being perilously close to poor-little-rich-prince territory.

"So we could have hit a few clubs in the evening," Saleh responded. "I don't see how any of that leads you to your decision to take this Mel to a holiday ball."

Ray sighed. "Also, her ex-husband will be attending. A very nasty man. She had no one to go with. She wants to prove to him that she's content without him."

Saleh nodded slowly, taking it in. "I see. So she has feelings for her former spouse."

"What? No. No, she doesn't." At least Ray didn't think she did.

"Then why would she care about what he thinks?"

It was a possibility Ray hadn't considered. He felt himself clench his fists at his sides. The idea rankled more than he would have thought.

Saleh continued, "I urge you to be careful. This is simply to be a brief reprieve, coupled with a business transaction. Do not forget you still have a duty to fulfill upon your return."

Ray turned to stare out the window. Traffic had slowed down and a light dusting of snow filled the air.

"I haven't forgotten."

CHAPTER FIVE

MEL DIDN'T COME to Newbury Street often. By far one of the ritziest neighborhoods in downtown Boston, it housed some of the city's most premier shops and restaurants, not to mention prime real estate. Many of New England's sports stars owned condos or apartments along the street. High-end sports cars, everything from Lamborghinis to classic Bentleys rolled down the pavement. Being December, the street was currently lined with faux mini Christmas trees, and big red bows adorned the old-fashioned streetlights.

When she did come out this way, it certainly wasn't to visit the type of boutique that she and Ray were about to enter. The type of boutique that always had at least one limousine sitting out front. Today there were two. And one sleek black freshly waxed town car.

When Ray had suggested going shopping,

she'd fully expected that they'd be heading to one of the major department stores in Cambridge or somewhere in Downtown Crossing.

Instead his friend Sal had picked her up and then dropped both her and Ray off here, at one of the most elite shops in New England. A place she'd only heard of. The sort of place where a well-heeled, well-manicured associate greeted you at the door and led you toward a sitting area while offering coffee and refreshments.

As soon as they sat down on the plush cushioned sofa and the saleslady walked away, Mel turned to Ray. "This is not what I had in mind. It's totally wrong. We shouldn't be here," she whispered.

Ray lifted one eyebrow. "Oh? There are a couple of other spots that were recommended to me. This was just the first one on the street. Would you like to continue on to one of those stores?"

He was totally missing the point. "No, that's not what I mean."

"Then I don't understand."

"Look at this place. It has to be beyond pricey.

This is the sort of place queens and princesses buy their attire."

Ray's face grew tight. Great. She had no doubt insulted him. Obviously he could afford such extravagance or whoever his acquaintance was wouldn't have recommended this to him.

"Please do not worry about the expense," he told her. "We have an agreement, remember?"

"But this is too much. I doubt I'd be able to afford so much as a scarf from a place like this." She looked down at her worn jeans and scruffy boots. It's a wonder the saleslady hadn't taken one look at her and shown her the door. If Ray wasn't by her side, no doubt she would have done exactly that.

"It's a good thing we are not in the market for a scarf today."

"You know what I mean, Ray."

"I see." He rubbed his chin, studied her. "Well, now that we're here, let's see what's available. Don't forget, we are not actually buying you a dress. It will go up for bidding at one of the queen's auctions, remember."

That was right. He had said that yesterday. When one considered it that way, under those conditions, it really didn't make sense for her to argue. Essentially, she was telling Ray how to spend his money and what to present to his queen. Who was she to do that? "I suppose it won't hurt to look."

As soon as she made the comment, the young lady who'd greeted them stepped back into the room.

"Miss, our designer has some items she would have you look at. Come right this way." With no small amount of trepidation, Mel followed her. She wasn't even sure quite how to act in a place like this. She certainly didn't feel dressed for the part. The slim, fashionable employee leading her down an elegant hall looked as if she'd walked straight off a fashion runway. Her tight-fitting pencil skirt and stiletto heels were more stylish than anything Mel owned.

The saleslady must have guessed at her nervousness. "Our designer is very nice. She'll love working with a figure such as yours. I'm sure there are several options that will look great on you."

Mel had the urge to give the other woman a

hug. Her kind words were actually serving to settle her nerves, though not by much.

"Thank you."

"I think your boyfriend will be very pleased with the final choice."

"Oh, he's not my boyfriend. We're attending an event together. Just as friends. And I had nothing to wear because I lost my bag. It's why I have this black eye and all this bruising—" She forced herself to stop talking and to take a deep breath. Now she was just rambling. "I'm sorry. I'm not used to seeing a designer to shop for a dress. This is all so unreal." She probably shouldn't have added that last part. Now the poor lady was going to think she was addled in addition to being talkative.

The other woman turned to her with a smile. "Then I think you should pretend."

"I don't understand."

"Pretend you are used to it."

Mel gave her head a shake. "How do I do that?"

She shrugged an elegant shoulder. "Pretend you belong here, that you come here often. And pretend he is your boyfriend." She gave her a small wink before escorting her inside a large dressing room with wall-to-wall mirrors and a big standing rack off to the side. On it hung a dozen dazzling evening gowns that took her breath away. And even from a distance, she could see none of them had a price tag. This wasn't the type of place where tags were necessary. Customers who frequented a boutique like this one knew they could afford whatever the mystery price was.

"Deena will be in to see you in just a moment."

With that, the greeter turned on her high, thin heels and left. All in all, her suggestion wasn't a bad one. Why shouldn't Mel enjoy herself here? Something like this was never going to happen to her again. What if she really was here on one of her regular shopping trips? What if this wasn't a completely novel experience and she knew exactly what she was doing? There was nothing wrong with enjoying a little fantasy. Lord knew she could use a bit of it in her life these days.

And what if the charming, devilishly handsome man sitting in the other room, waiting for her, really was her boyfriend?

Ray stared at the spreadsheet full of figures on his tablet, but it was hard to focus. If someone had told him a week ago that he'd be sitting in a fashion boutique in the heart of Boston, waiting for a woman to pick a gown, he would have laughed out loud at the notion. Not that he was a stranger to being dragged out to shop. He did have two sisters and a mother, after all. In fact, one of his sisters had been the one to suggest this particular boutique. Those two knew the top fashion spots in most major cities. The only problem was, now he was being hounded via text and voice mail about why it was that he needed the recommendation in the first place. He could only hold them off for so long. He would have to come up with an adequate response. And soon.

He felt Mel enter the room more than he heard her. The air seemed to change around him. When he looked up and saw her, his breath caught in his throat. The slim tablet he held nearly slipped out of his hands. Even with a nasty purple bruise on her cheek, she was breathtakingly stunning in the red gown. The color seemed to bring out every one of her striking features to their full effect.

Mel took a hesitant step toward him. She gestured to her midsection, indicating the gown she wore. "I wanted to see what you thought of this one," she said shyly.

He couldn't seem to get his tongue to work. He'd spent his life around some of the most beautiful women in the world. Everything from actresses to fashion models to noble ladies with royal titles. Yet he couldn't recall ever being this dumbstruck by a single one of them. What did that say about his sorry state of affairs?

"Do you think it will work?" Mel asked.

Think? Who would be able to think at such a moment? She could only be described as a vision, perhaps something out of a romantic fairy-tale movie. The dress hugged her curves in all the right places before flaring out ever so slightly below her hips. Strapless, it showed off the elegant curve of her necks and shoulders. And the color. A deep, rich red that not many women would be able to wear without the hue completely washing them out. But it only served to bring out the dark blue hint of her hair and accent the emerald green of her eyes. The fabric held a sheer hint of sparkle wherever the light hit it just so.

Since when had he become the type of man who noticed how an article of clothing brought out a woman's coloring or features?

He'd never felt such an urge to whistle in appreciation. Hardly suitable behavior for someone in his position.

What the hell, no one here actually knew who he was. He whistled.

A smile spread across Mel's face. "Does that mean you like it?"

Someone cleared their throat before Ray could answer. Sweet heavens, he hadn't even noticed the other woman in the room with them. She had a long tape measure hanging from her neck and gave him a knowing smile.

"This one was the top choice," the woman said. "If you're okay with it, we can start the necessary alterations."

He was way more than okay with it. That

dress belonged on Mel; there was no way they were walking out of here without it.

"I think it's perfect," he answered the designer, but his gaze was fixated on Mel's face as she spoke. Even with the angry purple bruising along her cheek and jaw and the black eye, she was absolutely stunning.

"Are you sure?" Mel asked. "If you'd like, I can show you some of the other ones."

Ray shook his head. He couldn't be more sure. "I have no doubt you'll be the most beautiful woman to grace that ballroom with that dress."

Mel ducked her head, but not before he noticed the pink that blossomed across her cheeks. "Even with my black eye?"

"I've never seen anyone look so lovely while sporting one."

"I'll be in the dressing room when you're ready, miss," the designer offered before leaving them.

Ray found himself stepping closer to her. He gently rubbed his finger down her cheek, from the corner of her eye down to her chin. "Does it still hurt very much?"

She visibly shivered at his touch, but she didn't pull away. In fact, she turned her face ever so slightly into his caress. It would be so easy for him to lean in closer, to gently brush her lips with his. She smelled of jasmine and rose, an intoxicating mix of scents that reminded him of the grand gardens of his palatial home.

He'd been trying to deny it, but he'd been thinking about kissing her since having breakfast with her. Hell, maybe he'd been thinking about it much before that. He had no doubt she would respond if he did. It was clear on her face, by the quickening of her breathing, the flush in her cheeks.

The loud honk of a vehicle outside pulled him out of his musings and back to his senses. He couldn't forget how temporary all this was. In a few short days, he would return to Verdovia and to the future that awaited him. One full of duty and responsibility and that would include a woman he wasn't in love with.

Love. For all the earthly privileges he'd been granted by virtue of birth, he would never know the luxury of falling in love with the woman he was to marry. He just had to accept that. He couldn't get carried away with some kind of fantasy while here in the United States. And he absolutely could not lead Mel on romantically. He had nothing to offer her. Other than a fun night celebrating the holiday season, while also proving something to her ex. That was all this whole charade was about.

With great reluctance, he made himself step away.

"You should probably go get the dress fitted and altered. I'll go settle the charge."

It took her a moment to speak. When she did, her voice was shaky. "So I guess we're really doing this, huh?"

"What exactly are you referring to?"

"Going to the ball together. I mean, once the dress is purchased, there'll be no turning back, will there?"

Ray could only nod. He had a nagging suspicion that already there would be no turning back.

Not as far as he was concerned.

CHAPTER SIX

As FAR AS transformations went, Mel figured she'd pulled off a major one. The image staring back at her in the mirror couldn't really be her. She hardly recognized the woman in the glass.

She was in Frannie and Greta's apartment. The two women had spent hours with her in order to get her ready. A lot of the time had been spent camouflaging the discolored bruising on her face. But the effect was amazing. These ladies knew how to use makeup to cover up flaws. Even upon close inspection, one would be hard-pressed to guess Mel had met the broadside of a set of steel handlebars only days before.

As far as soreness or pain, she was way too nervous to take any notice of it at the moment.

Her bosses had also helped do her hair in a classic updo at the crown of her head. Greta had found some sort of delicate silver strand that she'd discreetly woven around the curls. It only became visible when the light hit it just so. Exactly the way the silver accents in her dress did. Frannie had even managed to unearth some antique earrings that were studded with small diamond chips. They provided just enough sparkle to complement the overall look. All in all, the older women had done a notable job helping her prepare.

It was like having two fairy godmothers. Albeit very chatty ones. They'd both gone on incessantly about how beautiful Mel looked, how she should act flirty with Ray in order to get under Eric's skin and because they thought Ray was the type of man who definitely warranted flirtatious behavior. Mel had just stood silently, listening. The butterflies in her stomach were wreaking havoc and made it hard to just breathe, let alone form a coherent sentence.

She was trying desperately not to think about all the ways this night could turn into a complete disaster. Someone could easily ask a fairly innocuous question that neither Ray nor she had an adequate answer to. They'd never even discussed what story to tell about how they'd met or how long the two of them had known each other. The whole scenario was ripe for embarrassing mistakes. If Eric ever found out this was all some elaborate pretend date merely to prove to him that she'd moved on, he'd never let Mel live it down.

His fiancée would also have an absolute field day with the knowledge. Not to mention the utter embarrassment it would cause if her other acquaintances found out.

"I believe your ride is here," Frannie declared, peeking around the curtain to look outside.

Greta joined her sister at the window. She let out a shriek of appreciation. "It's a stretch."

"Not just any stretch," Frannie corrected. "A Bentley of some sort."

Greta gave her sister's arm a gentle shove. "Like *you* would know what a Bentway looks like."

"Bentley! And I know more than you, obviously."

The butterflies in Mel's stomach turned into warring pigeons. He was here. And he'd gone all out apparently, hiring a stretch limo. He so didn't need to do that. She'd never been quite so spoiled by someone before—certainly not by a man. If she wasn't careful, this could all easily go to her head. There would be no recovering from that. She had to remind herself throughout the night how unreal all of it was, how temporary and short-lived it would all be. Tomorrow morning, she'd go back to being Mel. The woman who had no real plans for her future, nothing really to look forward to until she managed to get back on her feet somehow. A task she had no clue how to accomplish just yet.

Taking a steadying breath, she rubbed her hand down her midsection.

"How do I look?"

The sisters turned to her and their faces simultaneously broke into wide grins. Was that a tear in Greta's eye?

"Like a princess."

The buzzer rang just then. "I guess I should head downstairs."

"I say you make him wait a bit," Frannie declared. "In the diner. It's not often our fine establishment gets a chance to entertain such an elegant, handsome gentleman in a well-tailored tuxedo."

"Not often?" Greta countered. "More like never."

That comment earned her a scowl from her sister. Mel slowly shook her head. "I think I should just get down there, before I lose all my nerve and back out completely." It was a very real possibility at this point. She wasn't sure she could actually go through with this. The more she thought about it, the more implausible it all seemed.

"Not a chance we would let you do that," both sisters said in unison with obvious fear that she actually might do such a thing.

Mel willed her pulse to steady. Slowly, she made her high-heeled feet move to the door. Without giving herself a chance to chicken out, she yanked it open to step out into the stairway. Only to come face-to-face with Ray.

"I hope you don't mind. The street door was open so I made my way upstairs." He handed her a single red rose. "It matches the color of your dress."

Mel opened her mouth to thank him but wasn't able to. Her mouth and tongue didn't seem to want to work. They'd gone dry at the sight of him. The dark fabric of his jacket brought out the jet-black of his hair and eyes. The way the man looked in a tuxedo could drive a girl to sin.

What had she got herself into?

The woman was a stunner. Ray assisted Mel into the limousine waiting at the curb as the driver held the door open for them. He had no doubt he'd be the most envied man at this soiree from the moment they entered. If he thought she'd looked beautiful in the shop, the completed product was enough to take his breath away. He would have to find a way to thank his sisters for recommending the boutique; they had certainly come through.

He had half a mind to ask the limo driver to turn around, take them to an intimate restaurant instead, where he could have Mel all to himself. And if that didn't make him a selfish cad, he didn't know what would. He had no right to her, none whatsoever. By this time tomorrow, he'd be walking out of her life for good. A pang of some strange sensation struck through his core at the thought. A sensation he didn't want to examine.

Within moments, they were pulling up to the front doors of the Boston World Trade Center grand auditorium. The aromatic fishy smell of Boston Harbor greeted them as soon as they exited the car. An attendee in a jolly elf hat and curly-toed shoes greeted them as they entered through the massive glass doors.

Mel suddenly stopped in her tracks, bringing them both to a halt.

"Is something the matter?" She'd gone slightly pale under the bright ceiling lights of the lobby. The notes of a bouncy rendition of "Jingle Bells" could be heard from the ballroom.

"I just need a moment before we walk in there."

"Take your time."

"I know this is no time to get cold feet," she began. "But I'm nervous about all that could go wrong."

He took her gently by the elbow and led her away from the main lobby, to a more private area by a large indoor decorative fountain. "I know it's not easy right now, but why don't you try to relax and maybe even have a good time?" She really did look very nervous.

"I'll try but… Maybe we should have rehearsed a few things."

"Rehearsed?"

"What if someone asks how we met? What will we say? Or how long we've known each other. We haven't talked about any of those things."

Ray took in the tight set of Mel's mouth, the nervous quivering of her chin. He should have been more sensitive to her possible concerns under these circumstances. He hadn't really given any of it much thought himself. As prince of Verdovia, he was used to being questioned and spoken to everywhere he went. As a result, he'd grown masterful at the art of delivering nonanswers. Of course, someone like Mel wouldn't be able to respond so easily.

He gave her elbow a reassuring squeeze. "I find that under situations like these, the closer one sticks to the truth, the better."

She blinked at him. "The truth? You want to tell them the truth?"

"That's right. Just not all of it. Not in its entirety."

"I'm gonna need an example of what you mean."

"Well, for instance, if someone asks how long we've known each other, we can tell them we've only met very recently and are still getting to know one another."

The tightness around her eyes lessened ever so slightly. "Huh. And if they ask for details?"

"Leave that part up to me. I'll be able to come up with something."

That earned him a grateful nod. "What if they ask about how we met?" She thought for a moment and then answered her own question. "I know, I can tell them I was knocked off my feet before I'd barely laid eyes on you."

He gave her a small laugh. "Excellent. See, you'll do fine." He offered her his arm and motioned with his head toward the ballroom entrance. When she took it, her grasp was tight and shaky. Mel was not a woman accustomed to even the slightest deception. But some of the tension along her jawline had visibly eased. Her lips were no longer trembling. Now, if he could just get her to smile, she might actually look like someone about to attend a party.

He slowly walked her to the ballroom. The decor inside had been fashioned to look like Santa's workshop in the North Pole. Large replicas of wooden toys adorned various spots in the room. A running toy train traveled along a circular track hanging from the ceiling. Several more staffers dressed up as elves greeted and mingled with the guests as they entered. Large leafy poinsettias served as centerpieces on each table.

"How about we start with some Christmas punch?" he asked Mel as he led her toward a long buffet table with a huge glass punch bowl in the center. On either side was a tower of glass flutes.

"I'd like that."

Ray poured hers first and handed her the glass of the bubbly drink. After grabbing a glass for himself, he lifted it in a toast. "Shall we toast to the evening as it's about to start?"

She tapped the rim of her glass to his. To his happy surprise, a small smile had finally graced her lips.

"I really don't know how to thank you for this, Ray. For all of it. The dress, the limo. That was above and beyond."

"It's my pleasure." It surprised him how true that statement was. They'd only just arrived and already he was having fun and enjoying all of it: the bouncy music, the fun decor. Her company.

"I wish there was some way I could really thank you. Aside from a diner meal, that is," she added, clearly disturbed. Ray had no doubt that even now she was racking her brain to come up with ways to "repay" him somehow. The concept was clearly very important to her.

He wanted to rub his fingers over her mouth, to soften the tight set of her lips with his touch. He wished there was a way to explain that she didn't owe him a thing. "Look at it this way, you're helping me to enjoy Boston during Christmastime. If it wasn't for you, Sal and I would just be wandering around, doing the same boring old touristy stuff I've done before."

Complete with a droll official tour guide and the promise of hours-long business meetings afterward. No, Ray much preferred the anonymity he was currently enjoying. Not to mention the delight of Mel's company.

"You have no idea how refreshing this all is," he told her.

Before Mel could respond, a grinning elf dressed all in green jumped in front of them. She held her hand whimsically above Mel's head. In her grasp was a small plant of some sort.

Mistletoe.

"You know what this means," the young lady said with a cheery laugh.

A sudden blush appeared on Mel's skin. She looked at him with question. "You needn't—" But he wasn't listening.

Ray didn't hesitate as he set his drink down and leaned closer to Mel. As if he could stop himself. What kind of gentleman would he be if he didn't kiss her under the mistletoe at a Christmas party?

They were no longer in a crowded ballroom. Mel's vision narrowed like a tunnel on the man across from her, the man leaning toward her.

Ray was about to kiss her, and nothing else in the world existed. Nothing and no one. Just the two of them.

How would he taste? What would his lips feel like against hers?

The reality was so much more than anything she could have imagined. Ray's lips were firm against hers, yet he kept the kiss gentle, like a soft caress against her mouth. He ran his knuckles softly down her cheek as he kissed her. She reached for him, ran her free hand along his chest and up to his shoulder. In response, he deepened the kiss. The taste of him nearly overwhelmed her.

But it was over all too soon. When Ray pulled away, the look in his eyes almost knocked the breath from her. Desire. He wanted her; his gaze left no doubt. The knowledge had her off balance. He was looking at her like he was ready to carry her off to an empty room somewhere. Heaven help her, she would let him if he tried. She gulped in some much-needed air. The mistletoe-wielding elf had left, though neither one of them had even noticed the woman walk away. How long had they stood there kissing like a couple of hormonal teenagers?

"Mel." He said her name like a soft breeze, his breath still hot against her cheek. She found herself tilting her head toward him once more. As foolish as it was given where they were, she wanted him to kiss her again. Right here. Right now.

He didn't get a chance. A familiar baritone voice suddenly interrupted them.

"Melinda? Is that you?"

Her ex-husband stood less than a foot away, staring at her with his mouth agape. He looked quite surprised. And not at all happy. Neither did the woman standing next to him. Talley, his new fiancée.

"Eric, hello." Mel flashed a smile in Talley's direction. "Talley."

Eric unabashedly looked her up and down. "You look nice, Mel." It was a nice enough compliment, but the way he said it did not sound flattering in the least. His tone was one of surprise. Ray cleared his throat next to her.

"Excuse my manners," Mel began. "This is Ray Alsab. He's visiting Boston on business."

Talley was doing some perusing for herself as the men shook hands. She seemed to appreciate what she saw in Ray. But who wouldn't? The man looked like something out of *Billionaire Bachelors* magazine.

"Is that so?" Eric asked. "What kind of business would that be?"

"Real estate." Ray answered simply.

"Huh. What exactly do you do in real estate, Ray?"

Mel wanted to tell him that it was none of his business, and exactly where he could go with his questions. But Ray gave him a polite smile. "I work for the royal government of Verdovia. It's a small island nation in the Mediterranean, off the Greco-Turkish coast. His Majesty King Farood is looking to expand our US holdings, including in Boston. I've been charged with locating a suitable property and starting the negotiations on his behalf."

Eric's eyebrows rose up to near his hairline. He gave a quick shake of his head. "I'm sorry, how does someone in that line of work know Mel?"

The condescension in his voice was so thick, Mel wanted to throw her drink in Eric's face.

But her date merely chuckled. "We met purely by accident." Ray turned to her and gave her a conspiratorial wink, as if sharing a private joke only the two of them would understand. Her laughter in response was a genuine reaction. The masterful way Ray was handling her ex-husband was a talent to behold.

"We'll have to tell you about it sometime," he continued. He then took Mel's drink from her and set it on the table. "But right now, this lady owes me a dance. If you'll please excuse us."

Without waiting for a response, he gently took Mel by the hand and walked with her to the dance floor.

Talley's voice sounded loudly behind them. "I wouldn't mind a dance, Eric. Remember, you promised."

"Nicely done, sir," Mel giggled as she stepped into Ray's arms. The scent of his skin and the warmth of his breath against her cheek sent tiny bolts of lightning through her middle.

"He's still staring. At you. The way he looks at you…" He let his sentence trail off, his hand on her lower back as he led her across the dance floor.

Mel could hardly focus on the dance. She was still enjoying how he'd just handled Eric. But the grim set of Ray's lips and the hardness in his eyes left no question that he was upset. Interactions with her ex often had that effect on people.

"He's just arrogant. It's one of his defining traits."

He shook his head. "It's more than that. He looks at you like he still has some sort of claim," Ray bit out. "As if you still belong to him." His tone distinctly told her that he didn't like it. Not in the least.

Mel had never been much for dancing, but she could hold her own with the steps. Plus, she'd done her fair share of clubbing in her university days. Having Ray as her partner however was a whole new experience. She felt as if she was floating on clouds the way he moved her around the dance floor, perfectly in tune with whatever beat the current song carried.

"You're a man of many talents, aren't you? Quite the talented dancer."

He tilted his head to acknowledge her compliment. "I started taking lessons at a very young age. My parents were real sticklers about certain things they wanted me to be proficient at. It's expected of the pr—" He suddenly cut off whatever he was about to say.

Mel didn't bother to ask for clarification. Whatever the reason, he was the most fluid dance partner a woman could ask for. Whether classic ballroom dances or modern holiday music, he moved like a man who was comfortable with himself. As the kids who ate at the diner would say, the man had the rhythm and the moves.

The impact of the unpleasant encounter with Eric was slowly beginning to ebb, and she decided to throw herself into this experience fully. Remembering what the assistant in the store had told her helped. Sometimes it was all right just to pretend.

And it wasn't exactly difficult to do just that as she leaned into his length once a slower song had begun to play. He was lean and fit, the hard muscles of his chest firm and hard against hers. It took all her will to resist leaning her head against his shoulder and wrapping her arms around his neck.

And she couldn't help where her mind kept circling back to: the way he'd kissed her. Dear heavens, if the man kissed like that while out in public in front of a crowd of partygoers, what was he like in private? Something told her that, if they hadn't come to their senses, the kiss might very well have lasted much longer, leading to a thrilling experience full of passion. Her mind went there, to a picture of the two of them. Alone. Locked in a tight embrace, his body up against hers. His hands slowly moving along her skin. A shiver ran all the way from her spine down to the soles of her feet.

Stop it!

That train of thought served no purpose. The man lived thousands of miles away, never mind the fact that he was part of a whole different world. Women like her didn't date millionaire businessmen. She had him for this one evening, and she'd make the most of it before he walked out of her life for good.

But someone had other plans. Eric approached from the side and tapped Ray on the shoulder. "May I cut in?"

Ray gave Mel a questioning look, making sure to catch her eye before answering. Mel gave him a slight nod. If she knew anything about her ex, he wasn't going to take no for an answer, not easily anyway. The last thing she wanted was some sort of scene, even a small one. Ray didn't deserve that. And neither did she.

"I'll just go refresh our glasses," Ray told her before letting her out of his arms and walking to the beverage table. "Come find me when you're ready."

Reluctantly, she stepped into the other man's embrace, though she made sure to keep as good a distance as possible. "This was one of your favorite Christmas carols," Eric commented as soon as Ray was out of earshot. "I remember very well."

He remembered wrong. The song currently in play was "Blue Christmas," one she wasn't even terribly fond of. He was confusing it with one she did like, "White Christmas." She didn't bother to correct him. She just wanted this dance to be over.

It was ironic really, how this evening was supposed to be about proving something to the man who currently held her in his arms. But right now, she didn't even want to give him a moment of her attention. In fact, all of her attention was currently fully focused on the dark, enigmatic man, waiting alone for her by the punch bowl. A giddy sense of pride washed over her at the thought. Authentic date or not, Ray was here with her. She could hardly wait to be dancing in his arms again.

Though judging by the looks several ladies were throwing in his direction, he might not be alone for long.

"So is he your boyfriend?" Eric asked with characteristic disregard for any semblance of propriety.

"We are getting to know each other," she answered curtly.

"Right. Is that what you were doing when we first walked in? It looked like you were getting to know his face with your lips."

That was more than enough. "Honestly, Eric.

I don't see how it's any of your business. We are divorced, remember?"

He winced ever so slightly. "Don't be that way, Mel. You know I still care about you. I don't want to see you get hurt."

"That's rich. Coming from you."

Eric let out a low whistle. "Harsh. But fair. You've grown a bit…let's say *harder*, in the past several months."

"I've had to grow in all sorts of ways since we parted."

"Just be careful, all right. That's all I'm saying." He glanced in Ray's direction. "Where's he from anyway? Exactly? *Vanderlia* doesn't ring a bell."

"Verdovia," she corrected. "We haven't really had a chance to discuss it." A sudden disquieting feeling blossomed in her chest. She really didn't know much about Ray's homeland. Why hadn't she thought to ask him more about where he was from?

"Why does it even matter, Eric?"

He shrugged. "Just trying to discover some more about your friend." He let go of her just long enough to depict air quotes as he said the last word. "He who's here to investigate potential properties and begin negotiations," he uttered the sentence in an exaggerated mimic of Ray's accent. Mel felt a surge of fury bolt through her core like lightning. Even for Eric, it was beyond the pale. Boorish and bordering on straight elitism.

"Are you actually making fun of the way he speaks?"

"Maybe."

Tears suddenly stung in her eyes. More than outrage, she felt an utter feeling of waste. How could she have given so much to this man? She wasn't even thinking of the money. She was thinking of her heart, of the years of her youth. He'd made it so clear repeatedly that he hadn't deserved any part of her. How had she not seen who he really was? She'd been so hurt, beyond broken, when he'd betrayed her with another woman and then left. Now she had to wonder if he hadn't done her an immense favor.

She pulled herself out of his grasp and took a steadying breath, trying to quell the shaking that had suddenly overtaken her. "I think I'm ready to go back to Ray now. I hope you and Talley have a great time tonight."

Turning on her heel, she left him standing alone on the dance floor. She wouldn't give him anything more, not even another minute of her time.

"You look like you could use some air," Ray suggested before she'd even come to a stop at his side. The grim expression in her eyes and the tight set of her lips told him her interaction with her ex-husband hadn't been all that pleasant. Not that he was surprised. He didn't appear to be a pleasant man in any way.

Which begged the question, how had someone like Mel ever ended up married to him in the first place? He was more curious about the answer than he had a right to be.

She nodded. "It's quite uncanny how well you know me after just a few days."

The comment was thrown out quite casually. But it gave him pause. The truth was, he *had* begun to read her, to pick up on her subtle vibes, the unspoken communications she allowed. Right now, he knew she needed to get away for a few minutes. Out of this ballroom.

"But first—" She reached for the drink he held and downed it all at once.

"It went that well, huh?"

She linked her arm with his. "Let's go breathe some fishy Boston air."

Within moments they were outside, behind the building, both leaning on a cold metal railing, overlooking the harbor. She'd certainly been right about the fishy smell. He didn't mind. He'd grown up near the Mediterranean and Black Sea.

And the company he was with at least made the unpleasant stench worthwhile.

The air held a crisp chill but could be considered mild for this time of year. Still, he shrugged off his jacket and held it out to her.

She accepted with a grateful nod and hugged the fabric around her. She looked good wearing his coat.

Mel drew out a shaky breath as she stared out over the water. "Hard to believe I was ever that naive. To actually think he was good husband material."

"You trusted the wrong person, Mel. You're hardly the first person to do so." His words mocked him. After all, here he was leading her to trust *him*, as well. When he wasn't being straight with her about who he was, his very identity. The charade was beginning to tear him up inside. How much longer would he be able to keep up the pretense? Because the longer it went on, the guiltier he felt.

"I should have seen who he really was. I have no excuses. It was just so hard to be alone all of a sudden. All my friends have moved away since graduation. On to bigger and better things."

He couldn't help but reach for her hand; it fitted so easily into his. Her skin felt soft and smooth to the touch. "What about extended family?"

Her lips tightened. "There's no one I really keep in touch with. Neither did my parents. It's been that way for as long as I can remember."

"Oh?"

"My father had no one. Grew up in foster homes. Got into quite a bit of trouble with the law before he grew up and turned his life around."

"That sounds quite commendable of him."

"Yeah. You'd think so. But his background is the reason my mother was estranged from her family. She came from a long line of Boston Brahmin blue bloods, who didn't approve of her marriage. They thought my father was only after her for their money. They never did come around. Not even decades of my parents being happy and committed could change their minds. Decades where neither one asked for a single penny."

Her declaration went a long way to explain her feelings about the hospital fee payment. No wonder she'd insisted on paying him back. It also explained her pushback and insistence on donating the dress, rather than keeping it.

"I never met any of them," she continued. "Supposedly, I have a grandmother and a few cousins scattered across the country."

He gave her hand a gentle squeeze. "I believe it's their loss for not having met you," he said with sincerity. It sounded so trite, but he whole-heartedly meant it.

"Thank you, Ray. I mean it. Thank you for all you've done tonight. And I'm sorry. I realize you haven't even had a chance to do any of the networking you had planned."

"I find myself caring less and less about that," he admitted.

She tilted her head and looked at him directly. "But it was your main reason for wanting to come."

"Not any longer."

She sucked in a short breath but didn't get a chance to respond. A commotion of laughter and singing from the plaza behind them drew both their attention. Several male voices were butchering a rendition of "Holly Jolly Christmas."

Ray turned to watch as about a dozen dancing men in Santa suits poured out of a party van and walked into one of the seafood restaurants.

He had to laugh at the sight. "You saw that, too, right? I haven't had too much of that champagne punch, have I?"

She gave him a playful smile and a sideways glance. "If it's the punch, then there's some strange ingredient in it that makes people see dancing Santas." She glanced at the jolly celebrators with a small laugh.

"Only in Boston, I guess."

She turned to face him directly. "You mentioned you wanted to experience the city, but not as a tourist. I may have an idea or two for you."

"Yeah? Consider me intrigued."

Ducking her chin, she hesitated before continuing, as if unsure. "If you have the time, I can show you some of the more interesting events and attractions. There's a lot to see and do this time of year."

He was more intrigued by the idea than he would have liked to admit. "Like my very own private tour guide?"

"Yes, it isn't much, but it would be a small thank-you on my behalf. For all that you've done to make this such a magical evening."

Ray knew he should turn her down, knew that accepting her offer would be the epitome of carelessness. Worse, he was being careless with someone who didn't deserve it in the least. Mel was still nursing her wounds from the way her marriage had dissolved and the heartless way her ex-husband had treated her. He couldn't risk damaging her heart any further by pursuing this charade any longer. This was supposed to be a onetime deal, just for one evening. To try to make up for the suffering and pain she'd endured after the accident he and Saleh had been indirectly responsible for.

But even as he made that argument to himself, he knew he couldn't turn down her offer. Not given the way she was looking at him right now, with expectation and—heaven help him—longing. He couldn't bring himself to look into her deep green eyes, sparkling like jewelry in the moonlight, and pretend he wasn't interested in spending more time with her. He might very well hate himself for it later, and Saleh was sure to read him the riot act. The other man was already quite cross with him, to begin with, about this whole trip. And especially about attending this ball. But Ray couldn't bring himself to pass on the chance to spend just one more day in Mel's company. Damn the consequences.

"That's the best offer I've had in a long

while," he answered after what he knew was too long of a pause. "I'd be honored if you'd show me around your great city."

CHAPTER SEVEN

"I DON'T SEE any frogs."

"You do realize it's mid-December, right?" Mel laughed at Ray's whimsical expression. He was clearly teasing her.

"I don't see any frozen frogs either."

"That's because they aren't here any longer. And if they were, they'd most definitely be frozen." She handed him the rented skates.

"But I thought you said we were going to a pond of frogs. Boston does have a very well-known aquarium."

"I figured you must have already been to the aquarium. And besides, they don't harbor any frogs there."

Okay. She obviously hadn't been very clear about exactly what they'd be doing. Mel had decided an authentic winter experience in Boston wouldn't be complete without a visit to the Frog Pond. It was the perfect afternoon for it:

sunny and clear, with the temperature hovering just near freezing. Not a snowflake to be seen. She'd figured they could start their excursion with a fun hour or so of skating, then they would walk around the Common, Boston's large inner-city park, which housed the ice rink in the center.

"I said we'd be going to the Frog Pond."

"So where are the frogs?" he asked, wanting to know.

"They're gone. This used to be a swampy pond years ago. But now it's a famous Boston attraction. During the hot summer months, it's used as a splashing pool. In the winter, it turns into an ice-skating rink. I figured it would be fun to get some air and exercise."

"I see." He took the skates from her hands and followed her to a nearby park bench to put them on. "Well, this ought to be interesting."

An alarming thought occurred to her. "Please tell me you know how to skate."

He sat down and started to unlace his leather boots. "I could tell you that. But I'd be lying to you."

Mel would have kicked herself if she could.

Why had she made such an assumption about a businessman from a Mediterranean island? She'd planned the whole day around this first excursion, neglecting to ask the most obvious question.

"Oh, no. I didn't realize. I'm so sor—"

He cut her off with a dismissive wave of her hand. "How difficult could it be? I'm very athletic, having played various sports since I could walk. I almost turned pro, remember?"

There was no hint of bragging or arrogance in his tone; he was simply stating a fact.

He motioned toward the rink with a jut of his chin. "If those tiny tots out there can do it, so can I."

Ray quickly proved he was a man of his word. After a couple of wobbly stumbles, where he managed to straighten himself just in time, he was able to smoothen his stride and even pick up some steam.

"Color me impressed," she told him as they circled around for the third time. That was all it took for Ray to complete a full pass around the rink without so much as a stumble. Just as he said, he'd been able to pick it up and had done so with a proficiency that defied logic. "I don't know if you're quite ready to a triple lutz in the center of the rink, but you seem to have got the hang of it."

He shrugged. "It's not all that different from skiing, really."

"Do you ski often?"

"Once or twice a year. My family owns an estate in the Swiss Alps."

Mel nearly lost her balance and toppled onto her face. An estate. In the Alps.

Not only was Ray a successful businessman in his own right—he would have to be to be working directly for the king of his nation—he came from the kind of family who owned estates. There was no doubt in her mind that there was probably more than just one.

Oh, yeah, she was so far out of her league, she might as well have taken a rocket ship to a different planet.

She was spared the need to respond when a group of school-age children carelessly barreled into her from the side. The impact sent her flying and threw her off balance. Unable to regain her footing, she braced herself for the impact of the hard ice. But it never came. Suddenly, a set of strong, hard arms reached around her middle to hold her steady.

"Whoa, there. Careful, love."

Love. Her heart pounded like a jackhammer in her chest, for reasons that had nothing to do with the startle of her near fall.

For countless moments, Mel allowed herself to just stand and indulge herself in the warmth of his arms, willing her pulse to slow. His breath was hot against her cheek. He hadn't bothered to shave or trim down his goatee this morning. The added length of facial hair only served to heighten his devilish handsomeness. She'd never been attracted to a man with a goatee before. On Ray, it was a complete turn-on. He managed to pull it off somehow in a sophisticated, classic sort of way.

"Thanks," she managed, gripping him below the shoulders for support. It was surprising that her tongue even functioned at the moment.

"Sure thing."

"I guess I should have thought this out more." In hindsight, ice-skating wasn't such a good idea, given that Ray hadn't even done it before and how disastrous it would be if she suffered another stumble. "Maybe I should have chosen a different activity."

He glanced down at her lips. "I'm very glad you did choose this. I'm enjoying it more than you can imagine."

She couldn't be misreading his double meaning. They were standing still in the outer ring of the rink, with other skaters whisking by them. The same group of kids skated by again and one of them snickered loudly as they passed. "Jeez, get a room."

Mel startled back to reality and reluctantly removed her hands from Ray's biceps. A quick glance around proved the kids weren't the only ones staring at them. An elderly couple skating together gave them subtle smiles as they went by.

How long had they been standing there that way? Obviously, it had been long enough to draw the attention of the other skaters.

"Just be careful," he said and slowly let go of her, but not before he tucked a stray strand of her hair under her knit cap. "We can't have you falling again. Not when your bruises appear to be healing so nicely."

She wanted to tell him it was too late. She was already off balance and falling in another, much more dangerous way.

They decided they'd had enough when the rink suddenly became too crowded as the afternoon wore on. Ray took Mel by the elbow and led her off the ice. In moments, they'd removed their skates and had settled on a park bench. Someone nearby had a portable speaker playing soulful R & B. Several middle school–age children ran around the park, pelting each other with snowballs.

All in all, it was one of the most relaxing and pleasurable mornings he'd spent. No one was paying the slightest attention to him, a rare experience where he was concerned. Mel sat next to him, tapping her leather-booted toe in tune with the music.

"Those kids have surprisingly good aim," he commented, watching one of the youngsters land a clumpy snowball directly on his friend's cheek. Mel laughed as the "victim" made an exaggerated show of falling dramatically to the snow-covered ground. After lying there for several seconds, the child spread out his arms and legs, then moved them up and down along the surface of the snow. He then stood and pointed at the snow angel he'd made, admiring his handiwork.

"I haven't made a snow angel in years," Mel stated, still watching the child.

"I haven't made one ever."

She turned to him with surprise clearly written on her expression. "You've never made a snow angel?" She sounded incredulous.

He shrugged. "We don't get that much snow in our part of the world. And when we're in the Alps, we're there to ski."

She stood suddenly, grabbing him by the arm and pulling him up with her. "Then today is the day we rectify that sad state of affairs."

Ray immediately started to protest. Anonymity was one thing, but he couldn't very well be frolicking on the ground, in the snow, like a playful tot. He planted his feet, grinding them both to a halt. "Uh, I don't think so."

Her smile faded. "Why not? You have to do

it at least once in your lifetime! What better place than the snow-covered field of Boston Common?"

He gave her a playful tap on the nose. "Making a snow angel is just going to have to be an experience I'll have to forgo."

She rolled her eyes with exaggeration. "Fine, suit yourself."

To his surprise, she strolled farther out into the park and dropped to the ground. She then lay flat on her back. He could only watch as she proceeded to make an impressive snow angel herself.

Ray clapped as she finished and sat on her bottom. "That's how it's done."

He walked over, reached out his hand to help her up.

And realized too late her sneaky intention. With surprising strength, she pulled him down to the ground with her.

"Now that you're down here, you may as well make one, too," she told him with a silly wiggle of her eyebrows.

What the hell? Ray obliged and earned a boisterous laugh for his efforts. By the time they stood, they were both laughing like children.

Suddenly, Mel's smile faltered and her eyes grew serious. She looked directly at him. "You didn't grow up like most boys, did you? Making snow angels and throwing snowballs at friends."

Her question gave him pause. In many ways, he had been a typical child. But in so many other aspects, he absolutely had not. "Yes. And no."

"What does that mean?"

"It means I had something of a very structured upbringing."

She studied him through narrowed eyes. "That sounds like you never got in any kind of trouble."

He shook his head. "On the contrary. I most definitely did."

"Tell me."

Ray brushed some of the snow off his coat as he gathered the memories. "Well, there was the time during my fifth birthday party when an animal act was brought in as the entertainment."

"What happened?"

"I insisted on handling the animals." Of course, he was allowed to. People didn't often turn down the request of the crown prince, even as a child.

"That doesn't sound so bad."

He bit back a smile at the memory. "There's more. See, I didn't like how the poor creatures were confined, so I set them free. Just let them loose in the garden. Several reptiles and some type of rodent."

Mel clapped a hand to her mouth and giggled at his words. Ray couldn't bring himself to laugh, for he vividly recalled what had happened in the immediate aftermath.

His father had pulled him into his office that evening as soon as he'd arrived home from a UN summit. Ray distinctly remembered that event as his first lesson on what it meant to be a prince. He was expected to be different from all the other children, to never make any mistakes. To never break the rules. He would always be held to a higher standard, as the world would always be watching him. It was a lesson that had stayed with him throughout the years.

On the rare occasions he'd forgotten, the repercussions had been swift and great.

"What about as a teen?" Mel asked, breaking into his thoughts.

The memory that question brought forth was much less laughable. "I got into a rather nasty fistfight on the field, during one particularly heated ball game. Walked away with a shiner that could compete with the one you've recently been sporting."

Mel bit her lip with concern.

"But you should have seen the other guy," he added with a wink.

Again, he wouldn't tell her the details—that the mishap had led to a near-international incident, where diplomats were called in to discuss at great length what had essentially been a typical teen tantrum over a bad play. As expected, the press had gone into a frenzy, with countless speculative articles about the king's lack of control over his only son and whether said son even had what it would take to be a competent king when the time came. His father had been less than happy with him. Worse, he'd been sorely disappointed. Yet another memorable lesson that had stayed with Ray over the years. Suddenly, the mood in the air had turned heavy and solemn.

"Come," Mel said after a silent pause, offering him her hand. "I think we could both use some hot cocoa."

He took her hand and followed where she led.

He hadn't been quite sure what to expect out of today. But Ray could readily admit it had been one of the most enjoyable days he'd ever spent. Now he stood next to Mel on the second level of Faneuil Hall, one of the city's better-known attractions.

"So this is Faneuil, then," he asked. He'd heard about the area several times during his research on Boston and on previous visits to Massachusetts. But he'd never actually had the chance to visit for himself. Until now.

"The one and only," Mel answered with a proud smile.

Ray let his gaze wander. He'd be hard-pressed to describe the place. It was an outdoor plaza of sorts, with countless shops, restaurants and pubs, all in one center area. But it was so much more. Several acts of entertainment performed throughout the square while adoring crowds clapped and cheered. Music sounded from every corner, some of it coming from live bands and some from state-of-the-art sound systems in the various establishments. Holiday decorations adorned the various shop fronts and streetlights. The place was full of activity and energy.

He and Mel had the perfect view of it all from above, where they stood.

"You're in for a real treat soon," Mel announced. "And we're in the perfect spot to see it." Even as she spoke, several people began to climb up the concrete steps to join them. Before long, a notable crowd had gathered.

"What kind of treat?"

She motioned with her chin toward the massive, tall fir tree standing on the first level. Even at this height, they had to look up to see the top of it. "They're about to light it in a few minutes. As soon as it gets dark."

They waited with patient silence as the night grew darker. Suddenly, the tree lit up. It had to have been decorated with a million lights and shiny ornaments.

Several observers cheered and clapped. Mel placed her fingers in her mouth and let out an impressive whistle.

"So what do you think?" she asked him after they'd simply stared and admired the sight for several moments. "I know Faneuil can be a bit overwhelming for some people."

Quite the opposite—he'd found it exciting and invigorating. "Believe it or not, it reminds me of Verdovia," he told her.

She glanced at him sideways, not tearing her gaze from the majestic sight of the tree as lights blinked and pulsed on its branches. "Yeah? How so?"

"In many ways, actually. We're a small country but a very diverse people. Given where we're located in the Mediterranean, throughout the years, settlers from many different cultures have relocated to call it home. From Central Europe to Eastern Europe to the Middle East. And many more." He motioned toward the lower level. "Similarly, there appears to be all sorts of different cultures represented here. I hear foreign music in addition to the English Christmas carols and American pop music. And it's obvious there are visitors here from all over the world."

Her eyes narrowed on the scene below in consideration of what he'd just told her. "I never thought of it that way. But you're right. I guess I just sort of took it all for granted. I've been coming here since I was a little girl."

"From now on, when you come, you can think about how it's a mini version of my home country."

Her smile faltered, her expression growing wistful. "Maybe I'll be able to see it someday."

Taking her hands, he turned her toward him. "I'd like that very much. To be able to show you all the beauty and wonder of my nation. The same way you've so graciously shown me around Boston."

"That'd be lovely, Ray. Really."

A wayward snowflake appeared out of nowhere and landed softly on her nose. Several more quickly followed, and before long, a steady flurry of snow filled the air.

Thick white flakes landed in Mel's hair, covering her dark curls. Ray inadvertently reached for her hair and brushed the snow off with his leathered fingers. He heard her sharp intake of breath at the contact.

Then she leaned in and surprised him with a kiss.

Stunned, he only hesitated for a moment. He wasn't made of stone, after all. Moving his hands to the small of her waist, he pulled her in closer, tight up against his length. She tasted like strawberries and the sweetest nectar.

He let her set the pace—she'd initiated the kiss, after all—letting her explore with her lips and tongue. And when she deepened the kiss and leaned in even tighter against him, he couldn't help but groan out loud. The touch and feel of her was wreaking havoc on his senses.

This was no way to behave. They were in public, for heaven's sake. What was it about this particular woman that had him behaving so irrationally? This was the second time in one day he'd wanted to ravage her in the plain view of countless strangers.

Grasping a strand of sanity, he forced himself to break the kiss and let her go. Like earlier at the ice-skating rink, they'd managed to attract the attention of observers.

"Mel."

She squeezed her eyes shut and gave a shake of her head. "I know. I'm sorry, I shouldn't have kissed you in public like that. Again. I can't seem to help myself."

"I believe the first kiss was my doing. But I had a mistletoe excuse."

She rubbed her mouth with the back of her hand and it took all his will not to take those lips with his own again. He really had to get a grip.

"Why don't we grab a bite?" he suggested, to somehow change the momentum and where this whole scenario might very well be headed: with him taking Mel behind one of the buildings and plundering her mouth with his. "The least I can do after you've entertained me all day is buy you dinner."

"I know just the place."

Within moments, they were down the stairs and seated at an outdoor eatery with numerous heat lamps to ward off the chill. Mel had chosen an authentic New England–style pub with raw shellfish and steaming bowls of clam chowder for them to start with.

Ray took one spoonful of the rich, creamy concoction and sighed with pleasure. He'd had seafood chowder before, but this was a whole new taste experience.

"This chowder is delicious," he told her.

"It's pronounced *chowdah* around here," she corrected him with a small laugh.

"Then this *chowdah* is delicious." Only, with his accent, he couldn't quite achieve the intended effect. The word came out sounding exactly as it was spelled.

Mel laughed at his attempt and then nodded in agreement. "It's very good. But I have to tell you, it doesn't compare to the chowder they serve in the town where I grew up. They somehow make it taste just a bit more home-style there. Must be the small-town charm that adds some extra flavor."

"You didn't grow up in the city?"

She shook her head. "No. About forty minutes away, in a coastal town called Newford. I moved to Boston for school and just ended up staying. Things didn't exactly turn out the way I'd intended after graduation, though."

The spectacle of her failed marriage hung unspoken in the air.

"Tell me more about your hometown," Ray prompted, in an attempt to steer the conversation from that very loaded topic.

A pleasant smile spread across her lips. "It was a wonderful place to grow up. Overlooking the ocean. Some of the small islands off the coast are so close, you can swim to them right from the town harbor. Full of artists and writers and creative free spirits."

"It sounds utterly charming."

She nodded with a look of pride. "It is. And we can boast that we have more art studios per block than most New England towns. One of which I could call a second home during my teen years, given all the hours I spent there."

That took him back a bit. "Really? At an art studio?" There was so much about her he didn't know.

"We had a neighbor who was a world-renowned sculptor. A master at creating magical pieces, using everything from clay to blown glass. He took me under his wing for a while to teach me. Said I had a real talent."

"Why haven't you pursued it? Aside from studying art history in college, that is."

She shrugged, her eyes softening. "I thought about maybe creating some pieces, to show in one of the galleries back home, if any of the owners liked them. But life got in the way."

Ray fought the urge to pull her chair closer to him and drape his arm around her. Her dreams had been crushed through no fault of her own. "Do you still see this sculptor who mentored you? Maybe he can offer some advice on how to take it up again."

Mel set her spoon down into her bowl. "Unfortunately, he passed away. These days, if I go back, it's only to visit an old friend of my mom's. She runs the only bed-and-breakfast in town. They also serve a chowder that would knock your socks off."

"I've never actually stayed at one of those. I hear they're quite charming."

"I'm not surprised you haven't frequented one. They're a much smaller version of the grand hotels your king probably likes to invest in. Tourists like them for the rustic feel while they're in town. It's meant to feel more like you're staying with family."

He was definitely intrigued by the prospect. A hotel stay that felt more like a family home. He would have to find time to stay in one on his next visit to New England. A pang of sorrow shot through his chest at that thought. He might very well be a married man at that time, unless he could convince the king otherwise. The idea made him lean closer to Mel over the table. He gripped his spoon tighter in order to keep from reaching for her.

Mel continued, "In fact, I should probably check in on her. The owner, I mean. Myrna has been struggling to make ends meet recently. She's on the market for a buyer or investor who'll take it off her hands and just let her run the place."

Ray's interest suddenly grew. The whole concept definitely called to him. But it wasn't the type of property the royal family of Verdovia would typically even take the time to look at. They'd never invested in anything smaller than an internationally known hotel in a high-end district of a major metropolitan city.

Still, he couldn't help but feel an odd curiosity about the possibilities. And wasn't he officially part of the royal family, who made such decisions?

CHAPTER EIGHT

"WHATEVER YOU'VE BEEN up to these past couple of days, I hope you've got it out of your system."

"And a good morning to you, as well." Ray flashed Saleh a wide smile as the two men sat down for coffee the next morning in the main restaurant of their hotel. Not even his friend's sullen attitude could dampen his bright mood this morning. Between the way he'd enjoyed himself yesterday with Mel and the decision he'd made upon awakening this morning, he was simply too content.

"Must I remind you that we're only here for a few more days and we haven't even inspected any of the hotels we've come out all this way to visit?" Saleh asked, pouring way too much cream into his mug. He chased it with three heaping spoonfuls of sugar, then stirred. How the man stayed so slim was a mystery.

"You're right, of course," Ray agreed. "At this point, we should probably split up the tasks at hand. Why don't you go visit two of the hotels on the list? I believe a couple of them are within a city block of each other."

"And what will you be doing, Rayhan? If you don't mind my asking," he added the last part in a tone dripping with sarcasm.

"I'll be visiting a prospect myself, in fact, if all goes as planned."

Saleh released a sigh of relief. "Better late than never, I guess, that you've finally come to your senses. Which one of those on the list would you prefer to check out?"

"It isn't on our list."

Saleh lifted an eyebrow in question. "Oh? Did you hear of yet another Boston hotel which may be looking for a buyout?"

"Not exactly. Though the place I have in mind is indeed interested in locating a buyer. Or so I'm told." He couldn't wait to run the idea by Mel, curious as to what her exact reaction might be. He hoped she'd feel as enthusiastic about the prospect as he did.

Saleh studied his face, as if missing a clue

that might be found in Ray's facial features. "I don't understand."

Ray took a bite of his toast before answering, though he wasn't terribly hungry after the large dinner he and Mel had shared the evening before. He'd definitely overindulged. The woman certainly knew what he might like to eat. In fact, after just a few short conversations, she already knew more about him than most people he'd call friends or family. He'd never quite divulged so much of himself to anyone before. Mel had a way of making him feel comfortable enough to talk about himself—his hopes, the dreams he'd once had. Around her, he felt more man and less prince. Definitely a new experience. He knew better than to try to explain any of it to the man sitting across the table. Best friend or not, he wouldn't understand. Ray couldn't quite entirely grasp what was happening himself.

"I'm considering, perhaps, looking at smaller options," he answered Saleh. "Something different than the grand international hotel chains."

"Smaller? How much smaller?"

"So small that the guests feel like they're actually staying with family."

Back to reality. Mel smoothed down the skirt of her waitress uniform and tried to force thoughts of Ray and the time they'd spent together yesterday out of her mind. Her shift would be starting in a few minutes and she had to try to focus. Customers really didn't like it when their orders were delayed, or if they mistakenly got the wrong dish.

It was time to pull her head out of the clouds. She'd done enough pretending these past few days.

"You look different," Greta declared, studying her up and down.

"Probably because my face is almost completely healed."

Frannie jumped in as she approached them from behind the counter. "No, that's not it. Greta's right. You look more—I don't know—sparkly."

Mel had to laugh. What in the world did she mean by that? "Sparkly?"

Both the older ladies nodded in unison. "Yeah,

like there's more brightness in your eyes. Your skin is all aglow. You even had a spring in your step when you walked in. Can't say I've seen you do that before."

Frannie suddenly gasped and slapped her hand across her mouth. "Dear sweetmeat! You said you were spending the day with that businessman. Please tell me you spent the night with him, too!"

Mel looked around her in horror. Frannie's statement had not been made in a low voice. Neither woman seemed to possess one.

"Of course not! We simply did some skating, walked for a bit around the Common and then had a meal together." Try as she might, Mel knew she couldn't quite keep the dreaminess out of her voice. For the whole day had been just that…something out of a dream. "He dropped me off at my apartment at the end of the evening like a true gentleman."

Greta humphed in disappointment. "Damn. That's too bad."

"You two know me better than that."

"We know you're due for some fun and excitement. You deserve it."

"And that you're not an old maid," the other sister interjected. "Not that there's anything wrong with being one."

"I think you should have seduced him!" Again, the outrageous statement was made in a booming, loud voice. Mel felt a blush creep into her cheeks. Though she couldn't be sure if it was from embarrassment or the notion of seducing Ray. A stream of images popped into her head that spread heat deep within her core, intensifying into a hot fire as she recalled how brazenly she'd kissed him on the walkway overlooking the tree above Faneuil.

"He's leaving in a few days, Greta."

Greta waved a hand in dismissal. "Lots of people have long-distance relationships. Think of how much you'll miss each other till you can see one another again."

"Thousands of miles away, along the Mediterranean coast, is quite a long distance," she countered, fighting back a sudden unexpected and unwelcome sting of tears. Just like her to be foolish enough to go and fall so hard for a man who didn't even live on the same continent.

Not that it really mattered. Where they each

lived was beyond the concept of a moot point. The fantasy of Ray was all well and good. But they weren't the type of people who would ever end up together in the long term.

Her family had never owned a European estate. What a laugh. She could barely afford the rent in her small studio apartment on the south side. She could only imagine how elegant and sophisticated Ray's parents and sisters had to be. Mel didn't even want to speculate about what they might think of someone like her. Look at the way her own father had been treated by his wife's family.

"So have some fun in the meantime," Greta argued. "He's still got a few more days in the States, you said."

"And I repeat, you know me better than that. I'm not exactly the type who can indulge in a torrid and quick affair." Though if any man could tempt her into doing so, it would most certainly be the charming man with the brooding Mediterranean looks who'd haunted her dreams all last night.

"Then maybe he should be the one who tries to seduce you," Frannie declared, as if she'd come up with the entire solution to the whole issue. Mel could only sigh. They clearly had no intention of letting the matter drop. She really did have to keep repeating herself when it came to the Perlman sisters.

"I already mentioned he was a gentleman."

The pocket of her uniform suddenly lit up as her phone vibrated with an incoming call.

Her heart jumped to her throat when she saw whose number popped up on the screen. It was as if her thoughts had conjured him. With shaky fingers, she slid the icon to answer.

The nerves along her skin prickled with excitement when she heard his deep, silky voice. Oh, yeah, she had it pretty bad.

And had no idea what to do about it.

"I wanted to thank you again for taking me to so many wonderful spots yesterday." Ray's voice sounded smooth and rich over the tiny speaker.

Mel had to suppress the shudder of giddiness that washed over her. She realized just how anxious she'd been that he might not reach out to her again, despite his assurances last night that he'd be in touch before leaving the United

States. "I had a lot of fun, too," she said quietly into the phone. Greta and Frannie were unabashedly leaning over the counter to get close enough to hear her end of the conversation.

"Believe it or not, I'm calling to ask you for yet another favor," Ray said, surprising her. "One only you would be able to help me with."

"Of course," she answered immediately, and then realized that she should at least inquire what he was asking of her. "Um. What kind of favor?"

"You gave me an idea last night. One I'd like to pursue further to see if it might be worthwhile."

For the life of her, she couldn't imagine what he might be referring to. Was she forgetting a crucial part of the evening? Highly unlikely, considering she'd run every moment spent with him over and over in her mind since he'd left her. Every moment they'd spent together had replayed in her mind like mini movies during her sleepless night. She'd felt light-headed and euphoric, and she hadn't even had anything to drink last night.

"I did?"

"Yes. Are you free later today?"

For him? Most certainly. And it wasn't like she had an active social life to begin with. She could hardly wait to hear what he had in mind. "My shift ends at three today, after the lunch crowd. Will that work?" It was impossible to keep the joy and excitement out of her voice. Something about this man wreaked havoc on her emotions.

"It does. Perfectly."

Mel's heart pounded like a jackhammer in her chest. She'd be spending the afternoon with him. The next few hours couldn't go by fast enough.

"I'm glad. But I have to ask. What is this idea I gave you?"

She could hardly believe her ears as he explained. Her off-the-cuff remark about the bed-and-breakfast in Newford had apparently had more of an impact on him than she would have guessed. She'd actually forgotten all about it. Ray's proposal sent a thrill down her spine. By the time she slid her phone back into her pocket, her excitement was downright tangible.

"Well, what was that all about?" Frannie demanded to know. "From the dreamy look on your face, I'd say that was him calling. Tell us what he said."

"Yeah. Must have been something good," Greta added. "You look like you're about ready to jump out of your skin."

All in all, it was a pretty apt description.

"Why, Melinda Lucille Osmon, let me take a look at you! How long has it been, sweetie?"

Ray watched with amusement as a plump, short older woman with snow-white hair in a bun on top her head came around the check-in counter and took Mel's face into her palms. "Hi, Myrna. It's been way too long, I'd say."

"Now, why have you been such a stranger, young lady?"

"I have no excuses. I can only apologize."

"Well, all that matters is that you're here now. Will you be staying a few days?"

It was endearing how many little old ladies Mel had in her life who seemed to absolutely adore her. She might not have any more living blood relatives, but she seemed to have true family in the form of close friends. Ray wondered if she saw it that way.

Right now, this particular friend was making a heroic effort to avoid glancing in his direction. No doubt waiting for Mel to introduce him and divulge what they were doing there together on the spur of the moment.

Not too hard to guess what conclusion the woman had jumped to about the two of them arriving at the bed-and-breakfast together. The situation was bound to be tricky. Both he and Mel had agreed on the ride over that they wouldn't mention Ray's intentions about a potential purchase. Mel didn't want to get the other woman's hopes up in case none of it came to fruition.

Mel hesitantly cleared her throat and motioned to him with her hand. "This is a friend of mine, Myrna. His name is Ray Alsab. He's traveling from overseas on business. He wanted to see an authentic bed-and-breakfast before leaving the States."

"Why, I'm honored that mine is the one he'll be seeing," the other woman said with a polite smile.

Ray reached over and took her hand and then planted a small kiss on the back, as was customary in his country when meeting older women. "The honor is all mine, ma'am."

Myrna actually fanned herself. "Well, you two happen to have great timing. It's the night of the annual town Christmas jamboree. To be held right here in our main room."

Ray gave Mel a questioning look. "It's a yearly get-together for the whole town," Mel began to explain. "With plenty of food, drink and dancing."

"Another ball, then?"

Myrna giggled next to him. "Oh, no. It's most definitely not a ball. Nothing like it. Much less fancy. Just some good old-fashioned food and fun among neighbors." She turned to Mel, her expression quite serious. "I hope you two can stay."

This time it was Mel's turn to give him a questioning look. She wasn't going to answer without making sure it was all right with him. *Why not*, Ray thought. After all, the whole reason he was here was to observe the workings and attraction of a small-town lodge. To see if it might make for a worthwhile investment.

Yeah, right. And it had absolutely nothing to do with how it gave him another excuse to spend some more time with Mel. He gave her a slight nod of agreement.

"We'd love to stay and attend, Myrna. Thank you."

Myrna clasped her hands in front of her chest. "Excellent. Festivities start at seven o'clock sharp."

"We'll be there."

"I'm so happy you're here. Now, let's get you two something to eat." She laid a hand on Mel's shoulder and started leading her down the hall. "Ruby's thrown together a mouthwatering beef stew, perfect for the cold evening." She turned to Ray. "Ruby's our head cook. She does a fine job."

Ray politely nodded, but his mind was far from any thoughts of food. No, there was only one thought that popped into his head as he followed the two women into a dining area. That somehow he was lucky enough to get another chance to dance with Mel.

* * *

"So, what do you think of the place?" Mel asked him as he entered the main dining room of the Newford Inn with her at precisely 7:00 p.m.

"It's quite charming," Ray answered truthfully. The establishment was a far cry from the five-star city hotels that made up most of his family's resort holdings. But if he was to deviate from that model, the Newford Inn would be a fine choice to start with. It held a New England appeal, complete with naval decor and solid hardwood floors. And the chef had done an amazing job with the stew and fixings. He still couldn't believe just how much of it he'd had at dinner. But Myrna had put bowl after bowl in front of him and it had been too good to resist.

"I'm so glad to hear it." She gave him a genuine smile that pleased him much more than it should have.

"Mel? What are you doing here?"

They'd been approached by a tall, lanky man who appeared to be in his thirties. He had a fair complexion and was slightly balding at the top of his head. The smile he greeted Mel with held more question than friendliness.

"Carl," Mel answered with a nod of her head. Her smile from a moment ago had faded completely.

"Wow, I wasn't expecting to see you here tonight."

"It was something of an unplanned last-minute decision."

The other man looked at Ray expectedly, then thrust his hand in his direction when Mel made no effort to introduce them. "I'm Carl Devlin. Mel and I knew each other growing up."

"Ray. Nice to meet you."

Carl studied him up and down. "Huh. Eric mentioned you were seeing someone," he said, clearly oblivious to just how rude he was being.

Mel stiffened next to him. "You and Eric still talk about me?"

Carl shrugged. "We talk about a lot of things. We're still fantasy-ball buddies."

Yet another American term Ray had never really understood the meaning of. It definitely didn't mean what it sounded like. As if American sports fans sat around together fantasizing about various sports events. Though, in a sense, he figured that was how the gambling game could be described.

Mel gave him a sugary smile that didn't seem quite genuine for her part either. "I'm so terribly happy that the two of you have remained friends since I introduced you two at the wedding. After all this time."

"Yeah. I'm really sorry things didn't work out between you two."

Ray felt the ire growing like a brewing storm within his chest. The blatant reminder that Mel had once belonged to a man who so completely hadn't deserved her was making him feel a strange emotion he didn't want to examine.

Luckily, Mel cut the exchange short at that point. She gently took Ray's arm and began to turn away. "Well, if you'll excuse us then, I wanted to introduce Ray to some friends."

Ray gave the other man a small nod as they walked away.

"I'm sorry if that was unpleasant," she said as she led him toward the other corner of the room. "I should have remembered that he and Eric still keep in touch."

"No need to apologize," he said and put his arm around her waist. "Though it occurs to me that we have the same predicament as we had the other evening at the holiday ball."

Her eyebrows lifted in question. "How so?"

"Looks like we'll have to put on a good show for your old friend Carl." He turned to face her. "Shall we get started?"

She responded by stepping into his embrace and giving him just the barest brush of a kiss on the lips.

CHAPTER NINE

"THIS MIGHT VERY well be the silliest dance I've ever done."

Mel couldn't contain her laughter as Ray tried to keep up with the line dance currently in play in the main room. Had she finally found the one thing Ray might not be good at? He was barely keeping up with the steps and had nearly tripped her up more than once when he'd danced right into her.

She had to appreciate the lengths he was going to simply to indulge her.

"You'll get the hang of it," she reassured him. "You're used to dancing at high-end balls and society events. Here at the Newford Inn, we're much more accustomed to doing the Electric Slide."

"It appears to be more complicated than any waltz," he said with so much grim seriousness that she almost felt sorry for him.

The song finally came to an end before Ray had even come close to mastering the steps. The next song that started up was a much slower love ballad. The dancers on the floor either took their leave and walked away, or immediately started to pair up. Ray reached for her hand. "May I?"

A shiver meandered down her spine. With no small amount of hesitation, she slowly stepped into his arms.

She wasn't sure if her heart could handle it. The lines between pretending to be a couple for Carl's benefit and the reality of her attraction to him were becoming increasingly blurry.

She had no doubt she was beginning to feel true and strong emotions for the man. But for his part, Ray's feelings were far from clear. Yes, he seemed to be doing everything to charm her socks off. But how much of that was just simply who he was? His charm and appeal seemed to be a natural extension of him. Was she reading too much into it all?

And that kiss they'd shared the night before while they'd watched the tree lighting. She'd felt that kiss over every inch of her body. She wanted to believe with all her heart that it had meant something to him as well, that it had affected him even half as much as it had affected her. The way he'd responded to her had definitely seemed real. There had been true passion and longing behind that kiss—she firmly believed that. But she couldn't ignore the fact that she'd initiated it. How many men wouldn't have responded? She didn't exactly have the best track record in general as far as men were concerned. Look at how badly she'd read Eric and his true intentions. In her desire to belong to some semblance of a family again, she'd gone ahead and made the error of a lifetime.

She couldn't afford to make any more such mistakes.

At the heart of it, there was only one thing that mattered. Ray would be gone for good in a few short days. She had to accept that. Only, there was no denying that he'd be taking a big part of her heart with him.

How foolish of her to let that happen.

Even as she thought so, she snuggled her cheek tighter against his chest, taking in the now-familiar, masculine scent of him. It felt right to be here, swaying in his arms to the romantic music.

Any hope she had that he might feel a genuine spark of affection died when he spoke his next words. "We definitely seem to have your friend Carl's attention. He seems convinced I can't keep my hands off you. If Eric asks, I'm sure he'll get the answer that we're very much enamored with each other."

Something seemed to snap in the vicinity of her chest. She yanked out of his arms, suddenly not caring how it would look. To Carl or anyone else.

"I don't care."

He blinked at her. "Beg your pardon?"

"I don't care what Eric thinks anymore. It was childish and silly to go through so much trouble just to prove a point to a selfish shell of a man." She swallowed past the lump that had suddenly formed in her throat. "A man I should have never fallen for, let alone married."

There was a sudden shift behind his eyes. He reached for her again and took her gently by the upper arms. "Come here."

Mel couldn't allow herself to cry. Since they'd

walked into the room, all eyes had been focused on them. There was zero doubt they were being watched still. It would be disastrous to cause a scene right here and now. The last thing she wanted was gossip to follow her on this visit.

She couldn't even explain why she was suddenly so emotional. Only that her heart was slowly shattering piece by piece every time she thought of how temporary this all was. A month from now, it would be nothing more than a memory. One she would cherish and revisit daily for as long as she lived. More than likely, the same could not be said for how Ray would remember her.

Or if he even would.

The thought made her want to sob, which would definitely cause a scene.

"Please, excuse me," she pleaded, then turned on her heel to flee the room. She ran into the outer hallway, making her way past the desk and toward the small sitting area by the fireplace. Ray's footsteps sounded behind her within moments. He reached her side as she stood staring at the crackling flames. She wasn't quite ready to turn and face him just yet.

"What's the matter, Mel?" he asked softly, his voice sounded like smooth silk against the backdrop of the howling gusts of wind outside.

She took too long to answer. Ray placed a gentle hand on her shoulder and turned her around. The concern in his eyes touched her to her core.

"Nothing. Let's just get back and enjoy the dancing." She tried to step to the side. "I guess I'm just being silly."

He wasn't buying it. He stopped her retreat by placing both hands on either side of her against the mantel. Soft shadows fell across his face from the light of the fire and the dim lighting in the room. With the heat of the flames at her back and that of his body so close to hers, she felt cocooned in warmth. Ray's warmth. Her stomach did a little quiver as he leaned closer.

"*Silly* is the last word I would use to describe you."

She wanted to ask him how he would describe her. What were his true, genuine thoughts as far as she was concerned?

The sudden flickering of the lights, followed by a complete blackout, served to yank her out of her daze. Now that the music from the other room had stopped, the harsh sound of the howling wind sang loudly in the air.

She'd been a New Englander her whole life and could guess what had just happened. The nor'easter storm forecast for much later tonight must have shifted and gained speed. The roads were probably closed or too treacherous to risk. Attempting the forty-minute ride back into Boston would be the equivalent of a death wish.

They were almost certainly snowbound for the night.

"I'm sorry, dear. Unfortunately, the one room is all I have. Between the holidays, the storm warnings and this annual holiday jamboree, we've been booked solid for days now. I only have the one small single due to a last-minute weather-related cancelation."

Mel had been afraid of that. She stood, speaking with Myrna in the middle of the Newford Inn's candlelit lobby. Most of the partygoers had slowly dispersed and headed back to their rooms or to their houses in town. Ray stood off to the side, staring in awe at the powerful storm blowing outside the big bay window. The power wasn't expected to come back on in the foreseeable future and Myrna's backup generators were barely keeping the heat flowing. "I understand. I'm not trying to be difficult. I hope you know that."

Myrna patted her hand gently. "Of course, dear." She then leaned over to her and spoke softly into her ear so that only Mel could hear her. "Are you scared in any way, dear? To be alone in a room with him? If you are, even a little bit, I'll figure something out."

Mel felt touched at her friend's concern. But fear was far from being the issue. She didn't know if she had the emotional stamina to spend a night alone in a small room with Ray.

She shook her head with a small smile. "No, Myrna. I'm not even remotely in fear of him. It's just that we haven't known each other that long."

"I'm so sorry, Mel," Myrna repeated. "Why don't you sleep with me in my room, then? It will be tight, but we can make do."

That offer was beyond generous. Mel knew Myrna occupied a space barely larger than a closet. Not to mention she looked beyond exhausted. Mel knew she must have been running around all day to prep for the jamboree. Then she'd had to deal with the sudden power outage and getting the heat restored before it got too cold. All on top of the fact that Mel and Ray hadn't been expected. She felt beyond guilty for causing the other woman any inconvenience.

Ray suddenly appeared at her side and gently pulled her to the corner of the room. "Mel, I must apologize. I feel responsible that you're stranded here. With me."

The number of people suddenly apologizing to her was beginning to get comical. All due to a storm no one could control or could have predicted.

Ray continued, "Please accept whatever room the inn has available for yourself. I'll be perfectly fine."

"But where will you sleep?"

He gave her hand a reassuring squeeze. "You don't need to concern yourself with that."

"I can't help it," she argued. "I am concerned." The only other option he had was the

SUV. "You're not suggesting you sleep in your car, are you?"

"It won't be so bad."

"Of course it will. You'd have to keep it running all night to avoid freezing. You probably don't even have enough gas to do that after our drive here."

"I can handle the cold," he told her. "I have roughed it in the past."

She quirked an eyebrow at him.

Ray crossed his hands in front of his chest. "I'll have you know that military service is a requirement in my country. I spent many months as a soldier training and surviving in worse conditions than the inside of an SUV during a storm. I can survive a few hours trying to sleep in one for one night."

He'd been a soldier? How much more was there about this man that she had no clue about?

Nevertheless, they had more pressing matters at the moment.

Mel shook her head vehemently. She couldn't allow him to sleep outside in a car during a nor'easter. Especially not in a coastal town. Plus, she felt more than a little responsible for their predicament. She was the native New Englander. If anything, she should have been prepared for the storm and the chance that it might hit sooner than forecast.

"Ray, setting aside your survival skills learned as a soldier, making you sleep outdoors is silly. We can share a room for one night."

He studied her face and then tipped his head slightly in acceptance. "If you insist."

She turned back to Myrna, glad to be done with the argument. What kind of person would she be if she allowed herself to sleep in a nice, comfortable bed while he was outside, bent at odd angles, trying to sleep all night in a vehicle? Military service or not.

"We'll take the room, Myrna. Thank you for your hospitality."

The other woman handed her an old-fashioned steel key. "Room 217. I hope you two stay warm."

"Thank you," she said with a forced smile, trying to convey a level of calm she most certainly didn't feel.

"Have a pleasant sleep," her friend added,

handing her two toothbrushes and a minuscule tube of toothpaste.

That was doubtful, Mel thought as she motioned for Ray to follow her. It was highly unlikely she'd get much sleep at all. Not in such close quarters with a man she was attracted to like no one else she'd ever met.

Not even the man she had once been married to.

Ray placed his hand on Mel's as she inserted the key to open the door to what would be their room for the night. "My offer still stands," he told her, giving her yet another chance to be certain. "I can go sleep outside in the vehicle. You don't need to do anything you're not completely comfortable with."

He'd never forgive himself for the predicament he'd just put Mel in. Who knew the weather along the northeastern coast could be so darn unpredictable? He wasn't used to accommodating unexpected whims of the forecast where he was from.

"I appreciate that, Ray. I do." She sighed and turned the key, pushing open the wooden door. "But we're both mature adults. I've spent enough time with you to know you're not a man to take advantage. Let's just get some sleep."

"You're sure?"

She nodded. "Yes. Completely."

Grateful for her answer—he really hadn't been looking forward to being sprawled out in the back seat of an SUV for hours in the middle of a storm—he followed her in. The room they entered wasn't even half the size of one of his closets back home in his personal wing of the castle. But the real problem was the bed. It was barely the size of a cot.

Mel must have been thinking along the same lines. Her eyes grew wide as they landed on it. He could have sworn he heard her swear under her breath.

"I'll sleep on the floor," he told her.

She immediately shook her head. "There's only the one comforter. That wouldn't be much better than sleeping in the car."

He took her by the shoulders and turned her to face him. "Again. I'm sorry for all of this. I can assure you that you can rest easy and fall asleep. I won't do anything to make you uncomfortable. You don't have to worry about that."

She gave him a tight nod before turning away. Again, she muttered something under her breath he couldn't quite make out.

Despite his unyielding attraction to her, he'd sooner cut off his arm than do anything to hurt her. It was hard to believe how much he'd come to care about her in just the short time since they'd met. She had to know that.

They both got ready for bed in awkward silence. Mel climbed in first and scooted so close to the wall she was practically smashed up against it. Ray got into bed and lay on his side, making sure to face the other way.

"Good night, Mel."

"Good night."

Wide-awake, he watched as the bedside clock slowly ticked away. The wind howled like a wild animal outside, occasionally rattling the singular window. Had Mel fallen asleep yet? The answer came when she spoke a few minutes later.

"This is silly," she said in a soft voice, almost

near to whispering. "I'm close to positive you aren't asleep either. Are you?"

Just to be funny, he didn't answer her right away. Several beats passed in awkward silence. Finally, he heard Mel utter a chagrined "Oh, dear."

He allowed himself a small chuckle, then flipped over onto his other side to face her. "Sorry, couldn't resist. You're right. I'm awake, too."

"Ha ha. Very funny." She gave him a useless shove on the shoulder. The playful motion sent her body closer against him for the briefest of seconds, and he had to catch his breath before he could speak again.

"I've never experienced a New England snowstorm before," he told her.

"It's called a nor'easter. We get one or two every winter, if we're lucky. If not, we get three, maybe even four."

"They're pretty. And pretty loud."

He felt her nodding agreement in the dark. "It can be hard to fall asleep, even if you're used to them."

"Since neither of us is sleeping," he began. "I was wondering about something."

"About what?"

"Something you said tonight."

"Yes?"

"When you told me you no longer cared about what Eric thought. Did you mean it?"

The sensation of her body so near to his, the scent of her filling his nostrils compelled him to ask the question. He realized he'd been wanting to all night, since she'd spoken the words as they'd danced together earlier.

He felt the mattress shift as she moved. "Yes. I did mean it. And I realize I haven't cared about his opinion for quite a while."

He wanted to ask her more, was beyond curious about what had led to their union. She seemed far too good for the man Eric appeared to be—she was too pure, too selfless. But this was her tale to tell. So he resisted the urge to push. Instead, he waited patiently, hoping she would continue if she so chose.

She eventually did. "I honestly don't know exactly what drew me to Eric. I can only say I'd suffered a terrible loss after my parents' passing. It's no excuse, I know."

"A person doesn't need an excuse for how they respond to grief," he told her.

"You speak as if you're someone who would know." She took a shaky breath. "Have you lost someone close to you?"

That wasn't it. He wouldn't be able to explain it to her. As the heir to the crown, he'd been to more ceremonial funerals than he cared to remember. Words had always failed him during those events, when confronted with the utter pain of loss that loved ones experienced.

"I haven't," he admitted. "I've been quite fortunate. I never knew my grandparents. Both sets passed away before I or my sisters were born."

She stayed silent for a while. "I lost the two most important people in the world to me within a span of a few months," she said, reminding him of their conversation from the other day. "I guess I longed for another bond, some type of tie with another person. So when Eric proposed..."

"You accepted." But she'd gone above and

beyond the commitment of her marital vows. "You also put him through school."

"I never wanted finances to be an issue in my marriage. Money was the reason I had no one else after my parents died."

"And you never fought to get any of it back? To get your life back on track or even to pursue your own dreams?"

He felt her tense up against him. Maybe he was getting too personal. Maybe it was the effect of the dark and quiet they found themselves in. Not to mention the tight and close quarters. But he found he really wanted to understand her reasoning. To understand *her*.

"It's hard to explain, really. I didn't have the stomach to fight for something I readily and voluntarily handed over."

"Is that the only reason?"

"What else?"

"Perhaps you're punishing yourself. Or maybe trying to prove that you can be independent and rebound. All on your own."

He felt her warm breath on his chest as she sighed long and deep. "I thought I was in love. To me, that meant a complete commitment.

Materially and emotionally." The statement didn't really answer his question. But he wasn't going to push.

She didn't need to explain anything to him. And he suddenly felt like a heel for making her relive her grief and her mistakes. Gently, softly, he rubbed his knuckles down her cheek. She turned her face into his touch and he had to force himself not to wrap his arms around her and pull her closer, tight up against him. As difficult as it was to do so, he held firm and steady without moving so much as a muscle. For he knew that if he so much as reached for her, it would be a mistake that could only lead to further temptation.

Temptation he wasn't sure he'd be able to control under the current circumstances.

Mel couldn't believe how much she was confiding about herself and her marriage. To Ray of all people—a man she'd just recently met and barely knew. But somehow she felt more comfortable talking to him than anyone else she could name.

She was curious about things in his past, also.

"What about you?" she asked, not entirely sure she really wanted to know the answer to what she was about to ask him. "There must have been at least one significant relationship in your past. Given all you have going for you."

"Not really. I have had my share of relationships. But none of them amounted to anything in the long run. Just some dear friendships I'm grateful for."

"I find that hard to believe."

He chuckled softly. The vibration of his voice sent little bolts of fire along her skin. "You can believe it."

"Not even at university? You must have dated while you were a student."

"Sure. But nothing that grew serious in any way."

She had no doubt the women he was referring to would have much rather preferred a completely different outcome. Ray seemed to have no idea the trail of broken hearts he must have left in his wake. Her eyes stung. She'd soon be added to that number.

After pausing for several moments, he finally continued, "I never really had much of a chance to invest any kind of time to cultivate the kind of relationship that leads to a significant commitment. As the oldest of the siblings, familial responsibilities far too often fell solely on my shoulders. Even while I was hundreds of miles away, studying in Geneva."

Ray sounded like he bore the weight of an entire nation on those shoulders. "Your family must be very important in Verdovia."

That comment, for some reason, had Ray cursing under his breath. "I'm sorry, Mel," he bit out. "For all of it."

He had to be referring to all the pain and anguish of her past that she'd just shared. Mel couldn't help but feel touched at his outrage on her behalf. The knowledge that he cared so deeply lulled her into a comfortable state of silence. Several moments went by as neither one spoke.

She wasn't sure how she was supposed to sleep when all she could think about was having Ray's lips on hers.

So it surprised her when she opened her eyes and looked at the clock, only to see that it read 7:30 a.m. A peaceful stillness greeted her as she glanced outside the window at the rising sun of early morning. The only sound in the room was the steady, rhythmic sound of Ray breathing softly next to her.

At some point, the winds had died down and both she and Ray had fallen asleep.

The air against her face felt frigid. Her breath formed a slight fog as she breathed out. The generators must not have been able to quite keep up with the weather, as the temperature in the room had gone down significantly. She came fully awake with a start as she realized exactly how she'd fallen asleep: tight against Ray's chest, snuggled securely in his arms. She hadn't even been aware of the cold.

CHAPTER TEN

THE AWKWARDNESS OF their position was going to be unbearable once Ray woke up. Mel racked her mind for a possible solution. She didn't even know what she would say to him if he woke to find her nestled up against his chest this way.

There was no doubt she'd been the one to do the nestling either. Ray remained in exactly the same spot he'd been when they'd got into the bed. She, on the other hand, was a good foot away from the wall.

She did the only thing she could think of. She pretended to snore. Loudly.

At first he only stirred. So she had to do it again.

This time, he jolted a bit and she immediately shut her eyes before he could open his. Several beats passed when she could hear him breathing under her ear. His body's reaction was nearly instantaneous. Heaven help her, so was her response. A wave of curling heat started in her belly and moved lower. Her fingers itched to reach for him, to pull him on top of her. Electricity shot through her veins at the images flooding her mind. She didn't dare move so much as an inch.

Mel heard him utter a soft curse under his breath. Then he slowly, gently untangled himself and sat up on the edge of the mattress. She felt his loss immediately. The warmth of his skin, the security of his embrace—if she were a braver, more reckless woman, she would have thrown all caution to the wind and reached for his shoulder. She would have pulled him back toward her and asked him for what she was yearning for so badly.

But Mel had never been that woman. Especially not since her divorce and the betrayal that had followed. If anything, the fiasco had made her grow even more guarded.

Ray sat still for several more moments. Finally, she felt his weight leave the mattress.

She wasn't proud of her mini deception, but what a relief that it had worked. The sound of the shower being turned on sounded from behind the bathroom door. There was probably no hot water. But Ray probably didn't need it.

She rubbed a shaky hand down her face. Hopefully he would take his time in there. It would take a while for her heart to steady, judging by the way it was pounding wildly in her chest.

Before long, the shower cut off and she heard him pull the curtain back.

Mel made sure to look away when Ray walked out of the bathroom, wearing nothing but a thick terry towel around his midsection. But it was no use, she'd seen just enough to have her imagination take over from there. A strong chiseled chest with just enough dark hair to make her fingers itch to run through it. He hadn't dried off completely, leaving small droplets of water glistening along his tanned skin. She had to get out of this room. The tight quarters with him so close by were wreaking havoc on her psyche. Not to mention her hormones. She sat upright along the edge of the mattress.

"You're awake," he announced.

She merely nodded.

"I…uh… I'll just get dressed."

"Okay." She couldn't quite meet him in the eye.

He began to turn back toward the bathroom.

"Do you want to take a walk with me?" she blurted out.

"A walk?"

"Yes. The wind and snow has stopped. We won't be able to start driving anywhere for a while yet. The salt trucks and plows are probably just now making a final run to clear the roads."

"I see. And all that gives you a desire to walk?" he asked with a small smirk of a smile gracing his lips.

"The aftermath of a snowstorm in this town can be visually stunning," she informed him. "I think you'd enjoy the sight of it."

He gave her an indulgent smile. "That sounds like a great idea, then."

She gave him a pleasant smile. "Great, you get dressed. I'll try to scrounge us up some coffee from the kitchen and meet you up front."

"I'll be there within ten minutes," he said with a dip of his head.

It was all the cue Mel needed to grab her coat and scarf, and then bolt out of the room.

As soon as she shut the door behind her, she leaned back against it and took several deep breaths. A walk was definitely an inspired idea. The air would do her good. And she knew just where to take him. Newford was home to yet another talented sculptor who put on a stunning display of three or four elaborate ice statues every year, right off the town square. At the very least, it would give them something to talk about, aside from the strange night they'd just spent in each other's arms.

But first, caffeine. She needed all the fortitude she could get her hands on.

Ray made sure to be true to his word and took the center staircase two steps at a time to find Mel waiting for him by the front doors. They appeared to be the only two people up and about—in this part of the hotel anyway.

"Ready?" she asked and handed him a travel mug of steaming hot liquid. The aroma of the rich coffee had his mouth watering in an instant.

He took the cup from her with a grateful nod

and then motioned with his free hand to the doors. "Lead the way."

He saw what she'd meant earlier as soon as they stepped outside. Every building, every structure, every tree and bush was completely covered in a thick blanket of white. He'd never seen so much snow in a city setting before, just on high, majestic mountains. This sight was one to behold.

"It looks like some sort of painting," he told her as they started walking. The sidewalks still remained thick with snow cover, but the main road had been plowed. He was thankful for the lined leather boots he was wearing. Mel was definitely more accustomed to this weather than he was. She maintained a steady gait and didn't even seem to notice the cold and brisk morning air. He studied her from the corner of his eye.

Her cheeks were flushed from the cold, her lips red and ripened from the hot brew she was drinking.

His mind inadvertently flashed back to the scene this morning. He'd awoken to find her snuggled tight in his embrace. Heaven help him, it had taken all the will he possessed to disentangle her soft, supple body away from his and leave the bed.

In another universe, upon waking up with her that way, he would have been the one to put that blush on her cheeks, to cause the swelling in those delicious ruby red lips.

He blinked away the thoughts and continued to follow her as she made her way to what appeared to be the center of town.

"Do we have a destination?" he asked, trying to focus on the activity at hand and not on the memory of how she'd felt nestled against him earlier.

"As a matter of fact, we do," she replied. "You'll see soon enough."

As he'd thought, they reached the center of town and what seemed to be some sort of town square. The sound of the ocean in the near distance grew louder the farther they walked. There was nothing to see in the square but more snow. How in the world would all this get cleaned up? It seemed an exorbitant amount. Where did it all go once it melted?

Verdovia's biggest snowstorm in the past decade or so had resulted in a mere light covering that had melted away within days.

"This way," Mel said.

Within moments, she'd led them to a small alleyway between two long brick buildings, a sort of square off to the side of the main square. In the center sat a now quiet water fountain of cherubic angels holding buckets.

But the true sight to behold was the handful of statues that surrounded the cherubs. Four large ice sculptures, each an impressive display of craftsmanship.

"Aren't they magnificent?" Mel asked him with a wide smile.

"Works of art," Ray said as they walked near to the closest one. A stallion on its hind legs, appearing to bray at the sky.

"They certainly are," Mel agreed. "This spot is blockaded enough by the buildings that the sculptures are mostly protected from the harsh wind or snow, even during nasty storms like the one last night," she explained.

True enough, all four of them looked none the worse for wear. He couldn't detect so much as a crack in some of the most delicate features, such as the horse's thick tail.

After admiring the statue for several moments, they moved on to the next piece. A mermaid lounging on a rock. The detail and attention on the piece was astounding. It looked like it could come to life at any moment.

"One person did all these?"

Mel nodded. "With some minor help from assistants. She does it every year. Arranges for large blocks of ice to be shipped in, then spends hours upon hours chiseling and shaping. From dusk till dawn. Regardless of how cold it gets."

He smiled at her. "You New Englanders are a hearty lot."

"She does it just for the enjoyment of the town."

"Remarkable," he said. Mel took him by the arm and led him a few feet to the next one.

"Take a look at this piece. This one's a repeat she does every time," she told him. "It's usually my favorite." She ducked her head slightly.

It was a couple dancing. That artist's talent was truly notable, she had managed to capture the elegance of a ballroom dance, even depicting an expression of sheer longing on the faces of the two entwined statues. With remarkable detail, the man's fingers were splayed on the small of the woman's back. She was arched on his other arm, head back atop a delicately sculpted throat. Icy tendrils of hair appeared to be blowing in the wind.

"She's really outdone herself with this one this year," Mel said, somewhat breathless as she studied the frozen couple.

Ray was beyond impressed himself. And he knew what Mel had to be thinking.

They'd danced that way together more than once now. He couldn't help but feel touched at the thought of it.

Mel echoed his thoughts. "It sort of reminds me of the holiday ball. I think you may have dipped me just like that once or twice."

Mel hadn't exaggerated when speaking of the artistic talent of her small town. These pieces were exquisitely done, even to his layman's eye. He'd never seen such artwork outside of a museum. Yet another memory he would never have gained had he never met the woman by his side.

He turned to her then. "I don't know how to thank you, Mel. This has truly been the most remarkable holiday season I've spent."

She blinked up at him, thrill and pleasure sparkling behind her bright green eyes, their hue somehow even more striking against the background of so much white. "Really? Do you mean that?"

"More so than you will ever know."

"Not even as a child?"

"Particularly not as a child."

She gripped his forearm with genuine concern. "I'm really sorry to hear that, Ray."

He took a deep breath. How would he explain it to her? That Christmas for him usually consisted of endless events and duties that left no time for any kind of appreciation for the holiday. By the time it was over, he was ready to send the yuletide off for good.

In just the span of a few short days, she'd managed to show him the excitement and appeal that most normal people felt during the season.

He was trying to find a way to tell her all of that when she surprised him by speaking again.

She took a deep breath first, as if trying to work up the courage.

"If you end up buying the Newford Inn," she began, "do you think you'll come back at all? You know, to check on your investment?"

The tone of her question sounded so full of hope. A hope he would have no choice but to shatter. He'd allowed this to happen. Mel was conjuring up scenarios in her head where the two of them would be able to meet up somehow going forward. Scenarios that couldn't have any basis in reality. And it was all his fault.

What had he done?

Ray might not have spoken the words, but his stunned silence at her question was all the answer Mel needed.

He had no intention of coming back here, regardless of whether he purchased the property or not. Not to check on an investment. And certainly not to see her. His expression made it very clear. Another thing made very clear was that he was uncomfortable and uneasy that she'd even brought up the possibility.

She'd done it again.

How much battering could a girl's pride take in one lifetime? If there was any way to suck back the words she'd just uttered, she would have gladly done so.

Foolish, foolish, foolish.

So it was all nothing but playacting on his part. She no longer had any doubt of that. Both at the ball and last night at the party. He'd never told her otherwise. She'd gone and made silly, girlish speculations that had no basis in reality.

"Mel," Ray uttered, taking a small step closer to her.

She held a hand up to stop him and backed away. "Please. Don't."

"Mel, if I could just try to ex—"

Cutting him off again, she said, "Just stop, Ray. It's really not necessary. You don't have to explain anything. Or even say anything. It was just a simple question. I'm sorry if it sounded loaded in any way with an ulterior motive. Or as if I was expecting anything of you with your answer."

Something hardened behind his eyes, and then a flash of anger. But she had to be imagining it. Because anger on his part would make no sense. He was the one rejecting her, after all.

"I didn't mean to imply," he simply stated.

"And neither did I."

She lifted her coffee cup and took a shaky swig, only to realize that the beverage had gone cold. The way her heart just had. Turning it over, she dumped the remaining contents onto the white snow at her feet. It made a nasty-looking puddle on the otherwise unblemished surface. Matched her mood perfectly.

"I appear to be out of coffee. I'd like to head back and get some more, please."

He bowed his head. "Certainly."

Suddenly they were being so formal with each other. As if they hadn't woken up in each other's embrace earlier this morning.

"And we should probably make our way back into Boston soon after. With our luck, another storm might hit." She tried to end the sentence with a chuckle, but the sound that erupted from her throat sounded anything but amused.

For his part, Ray looked uncomfortable and stiff. She had only herself to blame. The forty-minute ride back into the city was sure to be mired in awkward silence. So different from the easy camaraderie they'd enjoyed on the ride up. How drastically a few simple words could change reality overall. Words she had no business uttering.

The walk back to the hotel took much less time than the one to get to the statues, most of it spent in silence. In her haste, she almost slipped on a hidden patch of ice in the snow and Ray deftly reached out to catch her before she could fall. Tears stung her eyes in response to his touch, which she could feel even through her thick woolen coat. It was hard not to think of the way he'd spent the night touching her, holding her.

"Thanks," she uttered simply.

"You're welcome."

That was the bulk of their conversation until they reached the front doors of the bed-and-breakfast. Ray didn't go in; instead, he pulled the car keys out of his pocket. "I'll just go start the car and get it warmed up. Please, go get your coffee."

"You've seen all you need to see of the hotel, then?"

He nodded slowly. "I believe I have. Please thank Myrna for me if you see her. For all her hospitality and graciousness."

"I'll do that. It might take me a few minutes."

"Take your time. Just come down when you're ready."

Mel didn't bother to reply, just turned on her heel to open the door and step into the lobby. So it was that obvious that she needed some time to compose herself.

Clearly, she wasn't as talented at acting as Ray appeared to be.

CHAPTER ELEVEN

RAY REALLY NEEDED a few moments alone to compose himself.

He knew she was angry and hurt. And he knew he should let it go. But something within his soul just couldn't let the issue drop. He hadn't misread her intention when she'd asked about him returning to the United States sometime in the future. He couldn't have been that mistaken.

Regardless, one way or another, they had to clear the air.

Ray gripped the steering wheel tight as Mel entered the passenger seat and shut her door. Then he backed out of the parking spot and pulled onto the main road. It was going to be a very long ride if the silent awkwardness between them continued throughout the whole drive back.

She didn't so much as look in his direction.

They'd traveled several miles when he finally decided he'd had enough. Enough of the silence, enough of the tension, enough of all the unspoken thoughts between them.

He pulled off the expressway at the next exit.

"Where are we going?"

"I'd like a minute, if you don't mind."

She turned to him, eyes wide with concern. "Is everything all right? I can take over the driving if you'd like to rest your legs. I know you're not used to driving in such weather." Even in her ire, she was worried about his state. That fact only made him feel worse.

"It's not my legs," he said, then turned into an empty strip mall. The lone shop open was a vintage-looking coffee stop. "Did you mean what you said back in Newford? That you really don't expect anything of me?"

Mel stared at him for several beats before running her fingers along her forehead.

"Yes, Ray. I did. You really don't need to concern yourself." She let out a soft chuckle. "It really was a very innocuous question I asked back by the ice statues."

He studied her face. "Was it?"

"Absolutely."

He could prove her wrong so easily, he thought. If he leaned over to her right now, took her chin in his hand and pulled her face to his. Then if he plunged into her mouth with his tongue, tasted her the way he'd so badly wanted to this morning, it would take no time at all before she responded, moaning into his mouth as he thrust his fingers into her hair and deepened the kiss.

But that would make him a complete bastard.

She deserved better than the likes of him. The last thing he wanted was for her to feel hurt. Worse, to be the cause of her pain.

Instead, he sighed and turned back to look out the front windshield. "Well, good," he said. "That's good."

A small hatchback that had seen better days pulled up two spots over. The occupants looked at him and Mel curiously as they exited their car. It occurred to Ray just how out of place the sleek, foreign SUV must look in such a setting. Especially with two people just sitting inside as it idled in a mostly empty parking lot.

"Fine," Mel bit out.

She certainly didn't sound as if she thought things were fine. He inhaled deeply. "I'd like to clear the air, Mel, if I could. Starting with the bed-and-breakfast."

"What about it?"

"I should have been clearer about Verdovia's potential investment in such a property. Please understand. A small-town bed-and-breakfast would not be a typical venture for us. In fact, it would be a whole different addition to the overall portfolio of holdings. I would have to do extensive research into the pros and cons. And then, if the purchase is even feasible or even worth the time and effort, I'd have to do some real convincing. I haven't even run the idea by my fa—" He caught himself just in time. "I haven't run it by any of the decision makers on such matters. Most notably, the king and queen."

"I understand. That sounds like a lot of work."

"Please also understand one more thing—I have certain responsibilities. And many people to answer to." An entire island nation, in fact. "A certain level of behavior is expected of me. With a country so small, even the slightest deviation from the norms can do serious damage to the nation's sovereignty and socio-economic health."

He refrained from biting out a curse. Now he sounded like a lecturing professor. To her credit, Mel seemed to be listening intently, without any speculation.

He watched as she clenched her hands in her lap. "You can stop trying to explain, Ray. See, I do understand. In fact, I understand completely," she told him through gritted teeth. "You mean to say that I shouldn't get my hopes up. About the Newford Inn, I mean." Her double meaning was clear by the intense expression in her blazing green eyes and the hardened tone of her voice. "I also understand that Verdovia is much more accustomed to making bigger investments, and that nothing gets decided without the approval of the royal couple. Who have very high expectations of the man who obtains property and real estate on their behalf. Does that about sum it all up?"

Ray had to admire her thought process. It was as clear as day. She had just given him a perfect out, a perfect way to summarize exactly what he needed to say without any further awkwardness for either of them. He couldn't decide if he was relieved, annoyed or impressed. The woman was unlike anyone he'd ever met.

"I'm sorry." He simply apologized. And he truly was. She had no idea. The fate and well-being of an entire nation rested on his shoulders. To do what was best for Verdovia had been ingrained in him for as long as he could remember. He couldn't turn his back on that any more than he could turn his back on his very own flesh and blood. Verdovia needed a princess, someone who had been groomed and primed for such a position.

Even if he could change any of that, even if he turned to Mel and told her the complete truth about who he was at this very moment, then called his father and asked him to scrap the whole marriage idea, what good would any of it do?

Mel wasn't up to withstanding the type of scrutiny that any association with the Verdovian crown prince would bring into her life. Not many people could. If the international press even sniffed at a romantic involvement between Rayhan al Saibbi and an unknown Boston waitress, it would trigger a worldwide media frenzy. Mel's life would never be the same. He couldn't do that to her. Not after all that she'd been through.

He resisted the urge to slam his fist against the steering wheel and curse out loud in at least three different languages. The real frustration was that he couldn't explain any of that to her. All he had left were inadequate and empty apologies.

Mel finally spoke after several tense beats. "Thank you, but there's no need to say sorry. I'll get over it."

She turned to look out her side window. "And Myrna will be fine, too. The Newford Inn will find a way to continue and thrive. You said it yourself this morning. We New Englanders are a hearty lot."

Again, her double meaning was clear as the pure white snow piled up outside. With no small degree of reluctance, he pressed the button to start the ignition once more.

"I should get you home."

He had no idea what he would say to her or do once he got her there.

Mel plopped down on her bed and just stared at the swirl design on the ceiling. She felt as if she'd lived an entire year or two in the last twenty-four hours. Ray had just dropped her off and driven away. But not before he'd looked at her with some degree of expectation. She suspected he was waiting for her to invite him up so they could continue the conversation that had started when he'd pulled over to the side of the road.

She couldn't bring herself to do it. What more was there to discuss?

Not a thing. Once Ray left, she would simply return to her boring routine life and try to figure out what was next in store for her.

Easier said than done.

It occurred to her that she hadn't bothered to look at her cell phone all day. Not that she expected anything urgent that might need her immediate attention. Frannie and Greta weren't expecting her at the diner and no one else typically tried to contact her usually.

But this time, when she finally powered it on, the screen lit up with numerous text messages and voice mail notices. All of them from one person.

Eric.

Now what?

Against her better judgment, she read the latest text.

Call me, Mel. I'd really like to talk. I talked to Carl last night.

That figured. She should have seen this coming.

She had to admit to being somewhat surprised at his level of interest. He'd wasted no time after speaking with Carl to try to get more information out of her about the new man he thought she was seeing. What a blind fool she'd been where Eric was concerned. The man clearly had the maturity level of a grade-schooler.

No wonder she'd fallen for Ray after only having just met him.

But that was in itself just as foolish. More so. Because Ray wasn't the type of man a lady got over. Mel bit back a sob as she threw her arm over her face. Ray had certainly put her in her place during the car ride. He'd made it very clear that she should harbor no illusions about seeing him again.

She'd managed to hold it together and say all the right things, but inside she felt like a hole had opened up where her heart used to be.

She might have been able to convincingly act unaffected in front of Ray, but she certainly wasn't able to kid herself. She fallen head over heels for him, when he had no interest nor desire in seeing her again once his business wrapped up in the States.

She couldn't wallow in self-pity. She had to move on. Find something, anything that would take her mind off the magical days she'd spent with the most enigmatic and attractive man she was likely to ever meet.

She hadn't done anything creative or artistic in nearly two years. This might be an ideal time to ease herself back into using her natural talent for sculpting and creating something out of a shapeless slab of raw material. The idea of getting back into it sent a surge of nervous anticipation through the pit of her stomach.

She called up the keypad and dialed the number of the glass studio in Boston's Back Bay. A recorded voice prompted her to leave a message. She did so, requesting a date and time for use of the studio and materials. Then she made her way to the bathroom and hopped in the shower.

Studio time wasn't much in the way of adventurous, but at least it gave her some small thing to look forward to.

Her cell rang ten minutes later as she toweled off. Mel grabbed the phone, answering it without bothering to look at the screen. The studio had to be returning her call.

Mel realized her mistake as soon as she said hello. The caller wasn't the studio at all. It was her ex-husband.

"Mel? I've been calling you all day."

"What can I do for you, Eric?"

She had an urge to simply disconnect and hang up on him. She really was in no mood for this at the moment. But he'd simply keep calling and hassling her. Better to just have it out and get this over with.

"Carl called me last night. He mentioned you were visiting Newford. And that you weren't alone."

Well, he'd certainly gone and cut to the chase. Mel released a weary sigh. "That's right. I don't see how it's any of your business. Or Carl's, for that matter."

"I told you, Mel. I still care about you. We were man and wife once. That has to mean something."

"As much as it did the day you took off with your dental assistant, Eric?"

He let out an audible, weary sigh. "That's kind of why I'm calling. I've been giving this a lot of thought. I messed up, Mel. I shouldn't have walked away from our marriage."

What?

She nearly lost her grip on the phone. She had no idea where all this was coming from. But she had to nip it in the bud without delay. The whole idea of faking a pretend boyfriend in front of her ex-husband had backfired big-time. She'd simply meant to prove she'd moved on, and that she could attend a yearly event, even though he'd left her. The disaster happening right now hadn't even occurred to her as a remote possibility. Her ex-husband had made it more than clear two years ago that he had moved on and would be spending his life with another woman.

Or so Mel had thought.

She gripped the phone tight and spoke clearly. "Eric, you don't know what you're saying. I'm guessing you and Talley had a fight. And now you're simply overreacting."

He chuckled softly. "You're right about one thing."

"What's that?"

"We had a fight, all right. She became upset because I couldn't stop talking about you. And why you were with that businessman."

Mel had been ready to tell him the complete truth about Ray—she really had. If only just to end this nightmare of a phone call and return Eric's wayward thoughts back to where they belonged, to his wife-to-be.

But the way he said it, with such an insulting and derisive tone, made her change her mind.

She didn't owe this man anything, not an explanation, not any comfort. Nothing. Eric wasn't even worth her anger. He simply wasn't worth her time. No, she didn't owe him anything. But the truth was, he did owe *her*.

"Please, Mel. Can we just get together and talk?"

Ray's words from last night echoed in her mind. "Actually, maybe there is something we can talk about."

"Anything."

Mel figured he wouldn't be so enthusiastic once she brought up the subject matter. But Ray was right. She needed to stand up for herself and ask for what was rightfully hers. "I think we need to discuss some ways for you to pay me back, Eric. At least partially."

A notable silence ensued over the speaker. She'd shocked him.

She continued before he could say anything, "Other than that, you really need to stop concerning yourself with me and go resolve things with your fiancée. Now, if you'll excuse me, I'm waiting for an important phone call."

She didn't give him a chance to respond before continuing. "I wish you well, Eric," she said and meant it.

Then she disconnected the call.

CHAPTER TWELVE

MEL HUNG UP her apron and reached for her handbag atop the freestanding cabinet in the back kitchen. It had seemed a particularly long shift. Probably because she hadn't been able to focus on a thing to do with her job. Her mind kept replaying scenes from the past week over and over. Scenes which starred a handsome, dark-haired businessman who sported a shadow of a goatee on his chin and a smile that could charm a demon.

Hard to believe three days had gone by since Newford and the nor'easter that had stranded them overnight. It didn't help matters that she relived the entire experience every night in her dreams, as well as several times during the day in her imagination.

Suddenly Greta's scratchy voice sounded from the dining area. "Well, lookie who's here."

Mel's mouth went dry and her blood pounded

in her veins. She wasn't sure how, but she knew who her friend was referring to. *Ray.* He was here.

The suspicion was confirmed a moment later when Greta yelled yet again. "Mel, you should come out here. Someone to see you."

Mel threw her head back and closed her eyes. Taking a steadying breath, she grasped for some composure. She could do this. Even if the chances were high that he was simply here to tell her goodbye. For good.

Masking her emotions as best she could, she pushed open the swinging door and went out of the kitchen. Her breath stopped in her throat when she saw him. Again, he hadn't bothered with a coat. A crisp white shirt brought out the tanned color of his skin and emphasized his jet-black hair. His well-tailored dark gray pants fitted him like a glove.

She smoothed down the hem of her unflattering waitress uniform and went to approach him, her bag still clutched in her hands and a forced smile plastered on her face.

"Ray, I didn't expect to see you."

He jammed his hands in his pockets before

speaking. "I took a chance you may be at work. I was going to try your apartment if you weren't here."

"I see. Did you want to sit down?" As luck would have it, the only clean booth was the one they'd sat at together for breakfast that morning not so long ago—though now it seemed like another lifetime.

She'd been well on her way then, but hadn't yet quite fallen in love with him. Because that was exactly what had happened. She could no longer deny it. She'd fallen helplessly, hopelessly in love with Ray Alsab.

"I came to tell you that I've come to a decision. And it looks like we'll be moving forward."

She had to rack her brain to figure out exactly what he was talking about. Then it occurred to her. The bed-and-breakfast.

"You'll move forward with buying the Newford Inn, then?"

He nodded with a smile. "I wanted to tell you myself. We haven't even contacted Myrna yet."

Her heart fluttered in her chest, though whether it was the result of hearing the good news or seeing Ray's dashing smile again, she couldn't be sure.

"I've been speaking to all the appropriate people for the past three days," he added. "We've all decided to move ahead. The attorneys are drawing up the paperwork as we speak."

She was happy to hear it, she really was. Particularly for Myrna, who would have so much of the burden of owning the inn taken off her shoulders. But she couldn't just ignore the fact that all she wanted to do right now was to fling herself into his arms and ask him to take her lips with his own. Did he feel even a fraction the same?

It didn't appear so. Because here he was, and all he could talk about was the business deal he'd come to Boston for in the first place.

"It wouldn't have happened without you, Mel. I mean that. And this is just the start."

"The start?"

"That's the best part of it all. I told you the inn was much too small compared to Verdovia's hotel holdings. So we've decided to make it part of something bigger. We'll be investing in several more. A chain of resorts and inns throughout New England, all bearing the royal name. And you were the catalyst for it all."

She didn't know what to say. As much as she appreciated the credit he was giving her, all she could think about was how much she'd missed him these past few days, how she hadn't been able to get him out of her mind. There was no way she was going to tell him that, of course. But, dear heavens, she had to say something.

The words wouldn't form on her tongue, so she just sat there and continued to smile at him stupidly.

"Well, what do you think?" he finally prompted.

If he only knew.

"I think it's wonderful news, Ray. Really. I'm so glad it will work out. Sounds like your business trip will be a success. I'm happy for you."

His eyes suddenly grew serious. He reached across the table and took her hand in his. "There's something else I need to talk to you about."

Mel's pulse quickened and her vision suddenly grew narrow, her only focus at the moment being Ray's handsome face.

"I need to return home to get some things settled once and for all."

Mel felt the telltale stinging behind her eyes and willed the tears not to fall. She was right. This was simply a final goodbye. But his next words had her heart soaring with renewed hope.

"But then I'm going to call you, Mel. Once the dust is settled after I take care of a few things."

That was it, she couldn't hold back the tears, after all. He wasn't giving her the complete story, clearly, but neither was he shutting the door on the two of them. She would take it. With pleasure. She swiped at her eyes with the back of her arm, embarrassed at the loss of control.

He let out a soft chuckle and gripped her hand tighter. "Why are you crying, sweet Mel?"

She didn't get a chance to answer. Ray's phone lit up and vibrated in his front shirt pocket. With a sigh of resignation, he lifted it out. "I have to take this. I'm sorry, but it's about the inn and we're right in the middle of setting up the deal."

She nodded as he stood.

"I'll be right back."

Something nagged at the back of her mind as she watched Ray step outside to take the phone call. She'd got a brief look at the screen of his phone just now as his call had come through. The contact had clearly appeared on the screen as a call from someone he'd labeled as *Father*.

But he'd just told her the call was about the offer he was making to buy Myrna's bed-and-breakfast.

Why would his father be involved in a deal he was doing for the king?

Ray had never mentioned his father being in the same line of work. It didn't make any sense.

She gave her head a shake. Surely she was overthinking things. Still, the nagging voice continued in the back of her mind. The fact was, she'd had the same curious sense before. There seemed to be too many holes in the things Ray had told her about himself. Too many random pieces that didn't quite fit the overall puzzle.

She'd resisted looking at the questions too closely. Until now.

With trembling fingers, she reached into her

handbag for the mini electronic tablet she always carried with her to work and logged on to the diner Wi-Fi. Ray was still outside, speaking on the phone.

Mel clicked on the icon for the search engine.

Ray rushed back to the booth where Mel still sat waiting for him, anxious to get back to their conversation.

Something wasn't right. Mel's fists were both clenched tight on the table in front of her. Her lips were tight, and tension radiated off her whole body. One look at the screen on the tablet in front of her told him exactly why.

"Mel."

She didn't even bother to look up at him, keeping her eyes fixed firmly on what she was reading. Ray had never considered himself to be a violent man, save for that one youthful indiscretion on the ball field. But right now, he had a near-overwhelming desire to put his fist through a wall. The gossip rags never failed to amaze him with the unscrupulous ways they so often covered his life.

Mel had gone pale. She used her finger to

flip to another page on the screen. Ray didn't need to read the specific words to know what she was seeing. The international tabloid Mel currently stared at was a well-known one. One that featured him just often enough. Ray didn't bother lowering his voice as he bit out a vicious curse.

"Mel. Hear me out."

She still refused to look at him, just continued to read and then clasped a shaky hand to her mouth. Her gasp of horror sliced through his heart.

"Oh, my God," she said in a shaky whisper. "You don't just work for the royal family. You *are* the royal family."

"Mel." He could only repeat her name.

"You're the prince!" This time she raised her voice. So loud that the people around them turned to stare.

"It's what I was trying to explain." Even as he spoke, Ray knew it was no use. Too much damage had just been done. She was going to need time to process.

"When?" She pushed the tablet toward him with such an angry shove, it nearly skidded off the table before he caught it. "When exactly were you going to explain any of this?"

One particular bold headline declared that the Verdovian prince had finally chosen a bride and would be married within months. Somehow they'd snapped a picture of him with a young lady Ray didn't even recognize.

Damn.

"What's there to explain anyway?" she bit out through gritted teeth. "You lied to me. For days."

She was right. He'd been fooling himself, telling himself that not telling Mel the complete truth was somehow different from lying to her.

That itself was a lie.

He had no one to blame but himself. He rammed his hand through his hair and let out a grunt of frustration.

"Is it true?" she demanded to know. "That you're due to be engaged soon?"

He refused to lie yet again. "Yes."

"I need to get out of here," Mel cried out and stood. Turning on her heel with a sob that tore at his soul, she fled away from the table and toward the door.

Ray didn't try to chase after her. He didn't have the right.

And what would he tell her if he did catch up to her? That what she'd seen was inaccurate? The fact was he *was* the crown prince of Verdovia. And he had deceived her about it.

Greta and Frannie stood staring at him from across the room with their mouths agape. For that matter, the whole diner was staring.

"You'll make sure she's not alone tonight?" he asked neither sister in particular. They were both giving him comparably icy glares.

"You bet your royal patootie."

"Don't you worry about it," Frannie added. At least he thought it was Frannie. Not that it really mattered. All that mattered was that Mel was looked after tonight. Because of what he'd done to her.

As he left, Ray heard one of the diner patrons behind him.

"Told you this place was good," the man told his dining companion. "We got dinner and a show."

Ray was the prince. The actual heir to the crown. An heir who was due to marry a suitable, noble young woman to help him rule as king when the time came for him to take over the throne. Mel felt yet another shiver of shock and sorrow wash over her. Greta rubbed her shoulder from her position next to her on the couch. Frannie was fixing her a cup of tea in the kitchen. She didn't know what she'd do without these women.

"How could I have been so clueless, Greta?" she asked for what had to be the hundredth time. "How did I not even guess who he might have been?"

"How would you have guessed that, dearie? It's not every day a prince runs you over in the middle of a busy city street, then insists on buying you a dress to make up for it."

Mel almost laughed at her friend's summary. In truth, that accident had simply been the catalyst that had set all sorts of events in motion. Events she wasn't sure she would ever be able to recover from.

Her doorbell rang just as Frannie set a tray of cookies and steaming tea on the coffee table in front of them.

All three of them looked up in surprise. "Who could that be?"

Greta went over to look through the peephole. She turned back to them, eyes wide. "It's that fella that was with your prince. The one who was at the hospital that day."

Her prince. Only, he wasn't. And he never would be.

Mel's heart pounded at the announcement. "What could he possibly want?"

"Only one way to find out," Greta declared and then pulled open the door without so much as checking with Mel.

The gentleman stepped in and nodded to each of them in turn. He pulled an envelope out of his breast pocket.

"Sal?"

He gave her a slight bow. "My full name is Saleh. Saleh Tamsen."

Okay. "Well, what can I do for you, Mr. Saleh Tamsen?"

"It's more what I'm here to do for you," he informed her. What in the world was he talking about?

"The kingdom of Verdovia is indebted to you

for your recent service in pursuing a business contract. This belongs to you," he declared and then stretched his hand out in her direction.

Mel forced her mouth to close, then stood up from the couch and stepped over to him. He handed her the envelope. "What is it?"

"Please open it. I'm here to make sure you're satisfied and don't require a negotiation."

Negotiation? Curiosity piqued, Mel opened the envelope and then had to brace herself against Greta once she saw what it contained.

"Yowza!" Greta exclaimed beside her.

She held a check in her hand for an exorbitant sum. More money than she'd make waitressing for the next decade.

"I don't understand."

"A finder's fee. For bringing the prince to the Newford Inn, which he is in the process of acquiring on behalf of the king and the nation of Verdovia."

"A finder's fee? I hardly found it. I grew up near it." None of this made any kind of sense. Was this some type of inspired attempt on Ray's part to somehow make things up to her? That thought only served to spike her anger. If he was trying to buy her off, it was only adding salt to her wounds.

"Nevertheless, the check is yours."

Mel didn't need to hesitate. She stuck the check back in the envelope and handed it back to Saleh. "No, thank you."

He blinked and took a small step back. "No? I assure you it's standard. We employ people who do the very thing you accomplished. I can also assure you it's no more or less than they receive. Take it. You've earned the fee."

She shook her head and held the envelope out until he reluctantly took it. "Nevertheless, I can't accept this. Thank you, but no."

Saleh eyed her up and down, a quizzical gleam in his eye. "Fascinating. You won't accept the money, even though you've earned it."

"No, I won't. And please tell His Royal Highness I said it's not necessary."

Saleh rubbed his chin. "You know what? Why don't you just tell him yourself? He's waiting downstairs for me to return."

CHAPTER THIRTEEN

TO HIS CREDIT, Ray looked pretty miserable when he walked through her door. Though she doubted his misery could even compare to the way she was feeling inside—as if her heart had been pulled out of her chest, torn to shreds and then placed back inside.

Greta and Frannie had gone into the other room in order to give them some privacy. No doubt they had their ears tight against the wall, though, trying to hear every word.

Ray cleared his throat, standing statue still. "Mel. I didn't think you'd want to see me."

She didn't. And she did.

She gave him a small shrug. "It just didn't feel right. You know, leaving a prince waiting alone in a car. The last time I did that, at the inn, I didn't actually realize you were a prince. So you'll have to forgive me," she added in a voice dripping with sarcasm.

"You have every right to be upset."

If that wasn't the understatement of the century. "How could you, Ray?" She hated how shaky her voice sounded. "How could you have not even mentioned any of it? After all this time?"

He rubbed his forehead in a gesture so weary that it nearly had her reaching for him. She wouldn't, of course. Not now. Not ever again.

"It wasn't so straightforward. You have to understand. Things seldom are for someone in my position."

"Not even your name? You're Rayhan al Saibbi. Not Ray Alsab."

"But I am. It's an anglicized version of my name. I use it on business matters in North America quite often." He took a hesitant step toward her. "Mel, I never purposely lied to you."

"Those are merely semantics and you know it, Ray." She wanted to sob as she said the last word. She wasn't even sure what to call him now, despite what he was telling her about anglicized business aliases.

"It would have served no purpose to tell you, love. My confiding it all would have changed nothing. I'm still heir to the Verdovian throne. I still have the same duties that came with my name. None of my responsibilities would have changed. Nor would the expectations on me."

Mel had to gulp in a breath. Every word he uttered simply served to hammer another nail into her wound. She felt the telltale quiver in her chin, but forced the words. "The purpose it would have served is that I would have preferred to know all that before I went and fell in love with you!" Mel clasped a hand to her mouth as soon as she spoke the words. How could she have not contained herself? How could she have just blurted it out that way? Well, there was no taking it back now. And what did it matter anyway? What did any of it matter at this point?

Ray took a deep breath, looked down at his feet. When he tilted his head back up to gaze at her, a melancholy solace had settled in the depths of his eyes. "Then allow me to tell you the honest truth right now. All of it."

Mel wanted to run out of the room. She wasn't sure if she could handle anything he was about to tell her. Nothing would ever be the same again for her. No matter what he said right now. Her broken heart would never heal.

Ray continued, "The truth is that I completely enjoyed every moment you and I spent together. In fact, it might very well be the first time I actually spent a Christmas season having any fun whatsoever. In a different universe, a different reality, things would be very different between you and me. You are a bright light who also lights up everyone you're near. You certainly lit a light inside me. You should never forget that, Mel." He stepped over to her and rubbed the tip of his finger down her cheek in a gentle caress. "I assure you that I never will."

She couldn't hold on to her composure much longer. Mel knew she would break down right there in front of him if he said so much as one more word.

"I think you should leave now," she whispered harshly, resisting the urge to turn her cheek into his hand.

He gave her a slight tilt of his head. "As you desire."

She held back her tears right up until the

door closed behind him. Then she sank to the floor and simply let them fall.

"Well, that went about as well as could be expected."

Ray slid into the passenger side of the car and waited as Saleh pulled away and into traffic.

"Your lady is definitely not a pushover, as the Americans say."

Ray didn't bother to correct his friend. Mel certainly couldn't be referred to as his lady in any way. But he so badly wished for the description to be accurate.

"Did you even convince her to take the fee?" Saleh asked.

"No. I know there's no use. If she refused it from you, she will most definitely refuse it from me."

Saleh clicked his tongue. "Such a shame. The young lady is being stubborn at her own expense and detriment."

Ray nodded absentmindedly. He couldn't fully focus on Saleh's words right now. Not when he couldn't get Mel's face out of his mind's eye. The way she'd looked when she'd told him she'd fallen in love with him. What he wouldn't give to have the luxury of saying those words back to her.

But his friend kept right on talking. "Sometimes one should simply accept what he or she is owed. Or at least be adamant about asking for what they're owed, I would think. Don't you agree?"

Ray shifted to look at the other man's profile. "Is there a point you're trying to make?"

Saleh shrugged. "I simply mean to remind you that you are a prince, Rayhan. And that your father is the current ruling king."

"I think you should have taken the money!" Greta declared and popped one of the now-cold cookies into her mouth. The whole cookie. She started chewing around it and could hardly keep her mouth closed.

Frannie turned to her sister. "Why don't you go make us tea, Greta? It's your turn."

Greta gave a grunt of protest but stood and walked to the kitchen.

"You doin' all right, kid?" Frannie asked, taking Greta's place on the couch.

Mel leaned her head against the back of the couch and released a long sigh. "I don't know, honestly. It feels like there's a constant stabbing pain around the area of my heart and that it will never feel better." She sniffled like a child who'd just fallen and skinned her knee.

"It will. Just gonna take some time, that's all." Frannie patted Mel's arm affectionately. "Tell me something?"

"Sure."

"What's makin' you hurt more? That he didn't tell you who he was? Or that you can't have him?"

Mel blinked at the question. A friend like Frannie deserved complete honesty. Even if the question was just now forcing her to be honest with herself.

"I think you know the answer to that," she replied in a low, wobbly voice. Now that she was actually giving it some thought, she realized a crucial point: it was one thing when there had still been a chance for her and Ray, regardless of how miniscule. When she thought he was a businessman who might change his mind and return to the States because he couldn't bear to live without her. But he was a prince. Who had to marry someone worthy of one. Someone who was the polar opposite of a divorced, broke waitress who now lived in South Boston. It was almost exactly how her parents' relationship had started out. Only without the happy ending and loving marriage they'd shared.

"You didn't tell him that," Frannie declared. "You didn't even ask him how he felt. Don't you think you deserved to know? From his own mouth and in his own words, I mean?"

Mel closed her eyes. This conversation was making her think too hard about things she just wanted to forget. In fact, thinking at all simply made the hurt worse. "Well, as he pointed out himself, Frannie, none of it would have made any sort of difference." She knew her voice had taken on a snarky tone, but she couldn't summon the will to care. Hopefully the older woman would just drop the subject.

No such luck. Frannie let out a loud sigh. "Not so sure about that. Now, I may be old but I can count to two."

Mel gave her friend a confused look. "Is that some sort of South Boston anecdote?"

"All I'm saying is there appears to be at least two instances in your adult life where you didn't come out and ask for what was rightfully yours. Damn the consequences."

Mel couldn't be hearing this right. "You can't be including my ex-husband."

"Oh, but I am."

"Are you suggesting that I shouldn't have walked away from Eric? That I should have fought for him, despite his betrayal?" The question was a ridiculous one. She'd sooner have walked through the tundra in bare feet than give that man a second chance. Especially now, after these past few days with Ray.

Frannie waved her hand dismissively. "Oh, great heavens, no. Getting away from that scoundrel was the best thing that could have happened to you."

"Then what?"

Frannie studied her face. "He took your money, dear. Just took it and walked away with another woman."

"I gave him that money, Frannie. It was my foolish mistake."

"Your biggest mistake was trusting that he

would honor his vows and his commitment. He didn't."

Of course, the older woman had a valid point. But this train of conversation was doing nothing for her. She loved both Frannie and Greta, and she was beyond grateful for all the support and affection they'd consistently shown her. But Frannie had no idea what it was like to come home one day and find that your husband wouldn't be returning. That he'd found someone else, another woman he preferred over you. Frannie was a widow, whose husband had adored her right up until he'd taken his last breath. They'd had an idyllic marriage, much like her own parents'. The type of union that was sure to elude Mel, given her track record with men so far.

"Well, it just so happens I did ask Eric for the money back. At least some of it." Though she wasn't going to admit to her friend that it had been a half-hearted effort that was meant more to just get Eric off the phone the other night. And to make sure he didn't start harboring any illusions about the two of them reuniting in any way.

But Frannie had her figured out pretty well. Her next words confirmed it. "But you're not really going to fight for it, are you?"

Mel didn't bother to answer. She couldn't even think about Eric or what he owed her right now. Her thoughts were fully centered on Ray and the hurt of his betrayal.

"It's a cliché, but it's true," Frannie went on. "Some things are worth fighting for."

Mel clenched her hands. "And some fights are hardly worth it. They leave you bloodied and bruised with nothing to show for it."

"You might be right," Frannie admitted. "Matters of love can be impossible to predict, regardless of the circumstances. I'm just saying you should at least fight for what belongs to you." She nodded toward the door, as if Ray had just this instant walked out, rather than over two hours ago.

"And that man's heart belongs to you."

CHAPTER FOURTEEN

RAY COULDN'T REMEMBER the last time he'd tried to sleep in. He wasn't terribly good at it. But he felt zero incentive to get out of bed this morning. For the past few days, he'd awoken each morning with the prospect of seeing or at least speaking with Mel.

That wasn't the case today. And wouldn't be the case from now on. Hard to believe just how much he would miss something he'd only experienced for a short while.

His cell phone rang and his father's number flashed on the screen. He had half a mind to ignore it but couldn't quite bring himself to do so. In all fairness, he was way past the point where he owed the king a status report.

He picked up the phone. "Hello, Father."

"Good morning, son."

"Morning."

"Is there anything you'd like to tell me?"

So it was clear his father had heard something. Ray rolled onto his back with the phone at his ear. "Which tabloid should I be looking at?"

"Take your pick," his father answered. "There's some American man who claims to have been at something known as a 'jamboree,' where you were in attendance. Apparently, he took plenty of photos and is now selling them to whoever will pay."

Ray pinched the bridge of his nose. "I apologize, Your Majesty. I was conducting myself with the utmost discretion. But I failed to anticipate an unexpected variable."

"I see. I hope you've resolved the matter with the young lady in question."

"I'm working on it, sir."

His father paused for several beats before continuing, "You do realize the depth of your responsibilities to Verdovia, don't you, Rayhan? Don't lose sight of who you are. Loose ends will not be tolerated, son."

Ray felt a bolt of anger settle in his core. The way his father referred to Mel as a loose end had him clenching the phone tight in his hand.

He hadn't wanted to do this over the phone, but he'd come to a few decisions over the past few days. Decisions he wasn't ready to back away from.

"With all the respect you're due, Your Majesty, I feel compelled to argue that the lady in question is far from a loose end."

The king's sharp intake of breath was audible across the line. Ray could clearly picture him frowning into the phone with disappointment. So be it.

"I'm not sure what that means, son. Nor, frankly, do I care. I simply ask that you remain mindful of who you are and of your duties."

Ray took a deep, steadying breath. He'd been hoping to wrap things up here and have this conversation with his father in person. But fate appeared to be forcing his hand.

"Since we're discussing this now, Father, I wondered if we might have something of a conversation regarding duty and responsibility to the sovereign."

Silence once again. Ray couldn't remember a time he had tested the king's patience in such a manner. Nor his authority.

"What kind of conversation? What exactly is it you would like to communicate with me about responsibility and your honor-bound duties as prince?"

His father was throwing his words out as a challenge. Normally Ray would have been the dutiful, obedient son and simply acquiesced. But not this time. This time he felt the stakes too deeply.

"Thank you for asking, sir," Ray replied in his sincerest voice. "I'm glad to have an opportunity to explain."

His father sighed loudly once again. "If you must."

"I've been going over some numbers, sir."

"Numbers? What kind of numbers exactly?"

"I've been looking at our nation's holdings and overall wealth and how it impacts our citizens. Particularly since the time you yourself took over the throne. Followed by the growth experienced once I graduated university and began working for the royal house as a capitalist."

"And?" his father prompted. He sounded much less annoyed, less irritated. The discussion about figures and wealth had certainly gained his attention, just as Ray had known it would.

"And a simple analysis easily shows that the country has prospered very nicely since you started your reign, sir. And it continued that growth once I started acquiring investments on behalf of Verdovia. As a result, we've seen increased exports, higher wages overall for our citizens and extensions of most social benefits."

His father grunted, a sure sign that he was impressed. "Go on. Is there a point to all of this, son?"

"A simple point, sir. Maybe our duty shouldn't need to go any further than such considerations—to further the quality of life for our citizens and nationals. And that maybe we even owe a duty to ourselves as well, to ensure our own fulfillment and happiness. Despite being members of the royal house of al Saibbi."

Ray wouldn't blame her if she didn't open the door. He'd texted her last night to say he wanted to stop by this morning. She hadn't replied. Well, he was here anyway. On the off chance that she would give him one more opportunity and agree to see him.

The possibility of that seemed to lower with each passing second as he braced himself against the blowing wind, while standing on the concrete stoop outside her door.

He was just about to give up and turn around when he heard shuffling footsteps from the other side of the wood. Slowly, the lock unlatched and Mel opened the door.

She stepped aside to let him in.

"Thank you for seeing me, Mel. I know it's short notice."

She motioned toward the sofa in the center of the room. "I just brewed a pot of coffee. Can I get you some?"

"No. Thank you. I won't take up much of your time."

She walked over to the love seat across the sofa and sat as well, pulling her feet underneath her. Ray took a moment to study her. She looked weary, subdued. He saw no hint of the exuberant, playful woman he'd got a chance to know over the past week. He had no one but himself to blame for that.

"So you said you wanted to talk about a business matter? Do you have questions about the Newford Inn? If so, you could have called Myrna directly."

He shook his head. "This business matter involves you directly."

Her eyes scanned his face. "I hope you're not back to offer me another check. I told your associate I'm not interested in taking your money. Not when I didn't really do anything to earn it."

Ray leaned forward, braced his arms on his knees. "Well, we'll have to agree to disagree about whether you earned that money or not. But that's not why I'm here."

"Then why?"

"To put it simply—I'd like to offer you a position."

Mel's eyes narrowed on him, her gaze moving over his face. "Come again? Aren't you a royal prince, who'll eventually become king? What kind of position would someone like that offer a waitress?"

It was a valid question. "I am. The royal house is the largest employer in Verdovia. And a good chunk of the surrounding nations, in fact."

"Okay. What's that got to do with me? I'm a waitress in a diner."

At that comment, he wanted to take her by the shoulders and give her a mild shake. She was so much more than that.

"I mentioned to you earlier, that day at the diner, that we were looking to purchase several New England inns and B and Bs. I'd like to charge you with that. Your official title would be project manager."

Mel inhaled deeply and looked off to the side. "You're offering me a job? Is that it?"

He nodded. "Yes, I think you'd be perfect for it. You know the way these establishments operate and you know New England. The first part will be to get the Newford Inn purchased and renovated. That will give you a chance to slowly get your feet wet. What better way to ease into the job?"

When she returned her gaze to his face, a hardened glint appeared in her eyes. "It sounds ideal on the surface."

"But?"

"But I'm not sure what to tell you, Ray. What if you'd never accidentally met me that day?

Would I be the person you would think of to fill such a position?"

Ray gave her a small shrug. "It's a moot point, isn't it? The fact that we met is the only reason these deals are happening."

"I guess there's a certain logic in that," she agreed.

He pressed his case further. "Why worry about what-ifs? I need someone to assist with these acquisitions, and I think you'd do well."

She chewed the inside of her lip, clearly turning the matter over in her mind.

"Please, just think about it, Mel."

"Sure," she said and stood. "I'll think about it."

Something in her tone and facial expression told him she was simply humoring him. But he'd done what he could.

She walked him to the door.

He turned to her before she could open it. "Mel, please understand. Cultural changes don't happen quickly. Especially in a country so small and so set in its ways."

"You don't have to explain, Ray. I understand the reality of it all. You're here to offer me the only thing you feel you can. A job in your employ."

Damn it, when she put it that way…

"Thank you for stopping by. I promise to give your proposal a lot of consideration." She cracked an ironic smile that didn't quite reach her eyes. "After all, it's not like I'm all that great a waitress."

Mel watched through the small slit in her curtains as Ray walked down her front steps to the vehicle waiting for him outside. He hesitated before pulling the car door open and turned to stare at her building. It would be so easy to lift the window and yell at him to wait. She wanted to run out to him before he could drive away, to accept his offer, to tell him she'd take anything he was willing to give her.

But the self-preserving part of her prevailed and she forced herself to stay still where she was. Eventually, Ray got in and his car pulled away and drove off. She didn't even have any tears left; she was all cried out. In hindsight, she had to admit to herself that none of this was

Ray's doing. She was responsible for every last bit of it.

Melinda Osmon alone was responsible for not guarding her heart, for somehow managing to fall for a man so far out of her league, she wasn't even in the same stratosphere. To think, she'd believed him to be out of reach when she knew him as a businessman. Turned out he was a real live prince.

He'd had a point when he'd told her that he'd never lied to her outright. He'd never led her on, never behaved inappropriately in any way.

And he'd just shown up at her apartment with the offer of a job opportunity because he knew she was disappointed and defeated.

Mel leaned back against the window, then sank to her knees.

No. She had no one to blame but herself for all of it.

So now there was only one question that needed to be answered. What was she going to do about it? A part of her wanted so badly to take what she could get. To do anything she could to at least inhabit a spot in his orbit, however insignificant.

But that would destroy her. She wasn't wired that way. To have to watch him from a distance as he performed the duties of the throne, as he went about the business of being king one day.

As he committed himself to another woman.

And what of much later? Eventually, he would start a family with the lucky lady who ended up snaring him. Mel could never watch him become a father to someone else's children without shattering inside. Bad enough she would have to see it all from a distance.

Even the mere thought of it sent a stab of pain through her heart. She wouldn't survive having to watch it all from a front-row seat.

She knew Ray thought he'd found a workable solution. He'd offered her the only thing he could.

It just simply wasn't enough.

Ray sat staring at the same column of numbers he'd been staring at for the past twenty minutes before pushing the laptop away with frustration. He'd never had so much trouble focusing.

But right now, all he could think about was if he'd done the right thing by offering Mel a job.

He might very well have crossed a line. But the alternative had been to do nothing, to walk out of her life completely. At least as an employee of Verdovia's royal house, he could be confident that she was being taken care of, that she had the backing of his family name and that of his nation. It was the best he could do until he figured out what to do about everything else.

One thing was certain. He wasn't going to go along with any kind of sham engagement. If there was anything he'd learned during these past few days in the States, it was that he was unquestionably not ready. If that meant upsetting the council, the king and even the constituency, then so be it.

The sharp ring of the hotel phone pulled him out of his reverie. The front desk was calling to inform him there was some sort of package for him that they would bring up if it was a convenient time. Within moments of him accepting, a knock sounded on the door.

The bellhop handed him a small cardboard box. Probably some type of promotional material from the various endeavors he was currently involved in. He was ready to toss it aside when the return address caught his eye.

Mel had sent him something.

With shaky fingers, he pulled the cardboard apart. He couldn't even begin to guess what the item might be. She still hadn't given him any kind of answer about the job.

The box contained a lush velvet satchel. He reached inside the bag and pulled out some type of glass figurine. A note was tied to it with a red satin ribbon, almost the identical color of the dress she'd worn the night of the mayor's charity ball. He carefully unwrapped the bow to remove the item.

And his breath caught in his throat.

A blown-glass sculpture of a couple dancing. It wasn't quite a replica of the one made of ice they'd seen in the town square after the storm. She'd put her own creative spin on it. This couple was wrapped in a tighter embrace, heads closer together.

Her talent blew him away. She'd somehow captured a singular moment in time when they were on the dance floor together, a treasured moment he remembered vividly.

He gently fingered the smooth surface with his thumb before straightening out her note to read it.

Ray,
Though I can't bring myself to accept your offer, I hope that you'll accept this small gift from me. I didn't realize while creating it that it was meant for you, but there is no doubt in my mind now that you were the intended recipient all along.

I hope it serves as a cherished souvenir to help you to remember.

As I will never forget.

M

Ray gently set the figurine and the note on the desk and then walked over to the corner standing bar to pour himself a stiff drink. After swallowing it in one swig, he viciously launched the tumbler against the wall with all the anger and frustration pulsing through his whole being.

It did nothing to ease his fury.

CHAPTER FIFTEEN

RAY STILL HADN'T cleaned up the broken glass by the time room service showed up the next morning with his coffee tray. The server took a lingering look at the mess but wisely asked no questions.

"I'll get Housekeeping to clean that up for you, sir," the man informed him as Ray signed off on a tip.

"There's no rush. It can wait until their regular rounds."

"Yes, sir."

So he was surprised when there came another knock on the door in less than twenty minutes.

Ray walked to the door and yanked it open. "I said there was no hur—"

But it wasn't a hotel employee standing on the other side. Far from it.

"Mother? Father? What are you two doing here?"

His mother lifted an elegant eyebrow. "Aren't you going to invite us in, darling?"

Ray blinked the shock out of his eyes and stepped aside. "I apologize. Please, come in."

The queen gave him an affectionate peck on the cheek as she entered, while the king acknowledged him with a nod.

He spoke after entering the room. "Your mother grew quite restless with the girls away on their performance tour of Europe and you here in the States. She wanted to surprise you. So, surprise."

That it certainly was.

"How are you, dear?" his mother wanted to know. "You look a little ragged. Have you been getting enough sleep?"

Ray couldn't help but smile. Shelba al Saibbi might be a queen, but first and foremost she was a mother.

"I'm fine, Mother."

She didn't look convinced. "Really?"

"Really. But I can't help but think there must be more to this visit than your boredom or a simple desire to spring a surprise on your son."

He looked from one to the other, waiting for a response.

"Very well," his mother began. "Your father has something he needs to discuss with you. After giving the matter much thought."

The king motioned to the one of the leather chairs around the working desk. Ray waited until his father sat down before taking a seat himself. The queen stood behind her husband, placing both hands on his shoulders.

"What's this about, Your Majesty?"

"Saleh called me a couple of days ago," his father began. "He wanted to make sure I was aware of certain happenings since you've arrived in the US."

Ray felt a throb in his temple. Why, the little snitching...

His mother guessed where his thoughts were headed. "He did it for your own good, dear. He's been very concerned about you, it seems."

"He needn't have been."

"Nevertheless, he called and we're here."

"Does this have anything to do with your impending engagement?" his father asked.

Ray bolted out of the chair, his patience

stretched taut beyond its limits. Perhaps Saleh was right to be concerned about him. He'd never so much as raised his voice around his parents. "How can there be an engagement when I don't even really know the women I'm supposed to choose from? How can I simply tie myself to someone and simply hope that I grow fond of them later? What if it doesn't work out that way?" He took a deep breath before looking his father straight in the eye and continuing, "I can't do it. I'm sorry. I can't go forward with it. Even if means Councilman Riza continues to rabble-rouse, or that Verdovia no longer has the specter of a royal engagement to distract itself with."

"And what of your mother?" the king asked quietly, in a low, menacing voice.

Ray tried not to wince at the pang of guilt that shot through his chest. "Mother, I'm sorry. Maybe we can hire some more assistants to help you with your official duties. I can even take over some of the international visits myself. But I'm simply not ready to declare anyone a princess. I'm just now starting to figure out what type of relationship I might enjoy, the kind of woman I might want to spend my days with. It's not anyone back in Verdovia, I'm afraid."

His father stared at him in stunned silence. But to his utter shock, his mother's response was a wide, knowing grin.

"Well, goodness. You should have just told us that you've met someone."

Ray blinked at her. How could she possibly know that? Saleh might have called his parents out of concern, but Ray knew the other man would have never betrayed that much of a confidence.

"Is that so?" his father demanded to know. "Is all this turmoil because of that woman you were photographed dancing with?"

Ray forced himself to contain his ire. Not only were these people his parents, they were also his king and queen. "That woman's name is Melinda Osmon. And she happens to be the most dynamic, the most intriguing young lady I've ever met."

"I see." His father ran a hand down his face. "Is that your final say, then?"

Ray nodded. "I'm afraid so."

"You do realize that this will throw the whole country into a tailspin. Entire industries have been initiated based on speculation of an upcoming royal engagement and eventual wedding. Also, Councilman Riza will pounce on this as a clear and damning example of the royal family disappointing the people of Verdovia. A royal family he believes serves no real purpose and which is part of a system he believes should be abolished."

Ray swallowed and nodded. "I accept the consequences fully."

His mother stepped around the table to face her husband. "Farood, dear. You must think this through. We cannot have our only son bear the full brunt of this simply because he has no desire to be engaged. And we certainly can't have him miserable upon his return home."

She turned back to her son. "Do not worry about me, I can handle my duties just fine. Frankly, I'm getting a bit tired of all the fuss over my health. I'm not a fragile little doll that needs anyone's constant concern," she bit out, followed by a glare in her husband's direction.

Ray couldn't hide his smile. "I believe I've

come across stone blocks more fragile than you are, Mother."

The queen reached over and gave her son an affectionate pat. "I believe there's someone you need to go see, no?" She indicated her husband with a tilt of her head. "Do not worry about what this one will have to say about it."

For several moments, none of them spoke. A thick tension filled the air. Ray clenched his hands at his sides. The king had never been challenged quite so completely before. But he refused to back down.

It was what the Americans liked to call a "game of chicken." Finally, his father threw his hands up in exasperation. "I don't know what the two of you expect me to do about any of this."

The queen lifted her chin. "May I remind you, dear, that you are in fact the king?"

The statement echoed what Saleh had said to him all those nights ago.

His mother then added in a clipped tone, "I'm sure you'll think of something."

Mel tried not to turn her nose at the morning's breakfast special as she carried it out to the latest customer to order it. Lobster-and-cheese omelet. It appeared to be a big hit among the regulars, but for the life of her, she couldn't fathom why.

The holiday shoppers supplied a steady flow of patrons into the diner, despite the wintry cold. The forecasters were predicting one of the whitest Christmases on record. Though she'd be remembering this year's holiday herself for entirely different reasons. How would she ever cope with the Christmas season ever again when everything about it would forever remind her of her prince?

The door opened as several more customers entered, bringing with them a brisk gust of December wind and a good amount of snow on their covered boots and coats.

She nearly dropped the plates she was carrying as she realized one of those customers happened to be a handsome, snow-covered royal.

Mel couldn't help her first reaction upon seeing him. Though she hadn't forgotten the hurt and anguish of those few days, she'd realized she missed him. Deeply. She set her load down quickly in front of the diners before making a complete mess. Then she blinked to make sure she wasn't simply seeing what her heart so desperately wanted to see. But it really was him. He really was here.

Ray walked up to her with a smile. "Hey."

"Hey, yourself."

He peeled his leather gloves off as he spoke. "So I was hoping you could help me order an authentic New England breakfast. Any recommendations?"

She laughed, though she could barely hear him over the pounding in her ears. "Definitely not the day's special."

He tapped her playfully on the nose. "Should you be discouraging people from ordering that? You're right, you're not that great a waitress."

"What are you doing here, Ray? I thought you'd be heading back home. Myrna mentioned that the deal has already been settled and signed."

"I came to offer you a proposition."

Mel's heart sank. The happiness she'd felt just a few short moments ago fled like an elusive doe. He was simply here to make her some other kind of job offer.

"I'm afraid I'm still not interested," she told him in a shaky voice. "I should get back to work."

He took her by the arm before she could turn away. The touch of his hand on her skin set her soul on fire. She'd give anything to go back to the morning when she'd woken up in his arms at the inn. And to somehow suspend that moment forever in time.

She tried to quell the shaking in the pit of her stomach. Seeing him again was wreaking havoc on her equilibrium. But she refused to accept his crumbs. She'd made that mistake once already to avoid being alone, and she wouldn't do it again. Not even for this man.

"I can't do it, Ray. Please don't ask me to work for you again. I don't want your job opportunity."

He steadfastly held on to her arm. "Don't you want to hear what it is first?" he asked with a tease in his voice.

Something about the lightness in his tone and the twinkle in his dark eyes gave her pause. Ray was up to something.

"All right."

He tapped the finger of his free hand against his temple. "I've come up with it completely myself. A brand-new position, which involves a lot of travel. You'll be accompanying a certain royal member of Verdovia to various functions and events throughout the world. Maybe even a holiday ball or two."

He couldn't mean… She wouldn't allow herself to hope. Could she? "Is that so?"

He nodded with a grin. "Definitely."

Oh, yeah, he was definitely up to something. "What else?" she prompted, now unable to keep the excitement out of her voice. Was he really here to say he wanted to spend time with her? That he wanted to be with her? Or was it possible that she had not actually woken up yet this morning and was still in the midst of the most wonderful dream.

Ray rubbed his chin. "I almost forgot. There'll be a lot of this—" Before she could guess what he meant, he pulled her to him and took her lips with his own. The world stood still. Her hands moved up to his shoulders as she savored the taste of him. It had been so long.

She couldn't tear herself away, though a diner

full of people had to be watching them. This was all she'd been able to think about since the moment she'd first laid eyes on him on that Boston street.

Someone behind them whistled as another started a steady clap. Mel knew Greta and Frannie had to be the initiators of the cheers, but pretty soon the whole diner had joined in.

In response, Ray finally pulled away with a small chuckle and then twirled her around in a mini waltz around one of the empty tables in the center of the room.

"I miss dancing with you," he whispered against her ear and sent her heart near to bursting with joy.

The applause grew even louder. Catcalls and whistles loudly filled the air. But she could hardly hear any of it over the joyous pounding of her heart.

Ray dipped Mel in his arms in an elaborate ending to their mini waltz and gave her another quick kiss on the lips.

He turned to where Frannie and Greta stood over by the counter, grinning from ear to ear.

He gave them both a small nod, which they each returned with an exaggerated curtsy that almost had Greta toppling over.

"If it's not all that busy, would you mind if my lady here takes the rest of the day off?"

Their answer was a loud, resounding "Yes," which was said in unison.

Mel laughed in his arms as he straightened, bringing her back up with him.

"Get your coat and come with me before I have to carry you out of here."

Behind them, Ray heard a voice that sounded vaguely familiar. "I'm telling you, these guys should sell tickets. It's better than going to the movies."

The man was right. This was so much better than any movie. And Ray knew without a doubt there'd be a happy ending.

EPILOGUE

"THOSE TWO MAKE for the most unconventional bridesmaids in the history of weddings," Ray said, laughing, motioning across the room to where Greta and Frannie sat with his two sisters at the bridesmaids' table.

Mel returned his chuckle as she took in the sight of the four of them.

"One would think those four have known each other for years."

"They certainly don't seem to mind the vast age difference," Mel added with a laugh of her own.

Ray took her hand in his on top of the table and rubbed his thumb along the inside of her palm. A ripple of arousal ran over her skin and she had to suck in a breath at her instant reaction. The merest touch still set her on fire, even after all these months together.

"They're pretty unconventional in lots of

ways," she said with a smile, still trying to ignore the fluttering in her chest that was only getting stronger as Ray continued his soft caress of her hand.

Verdovia's version of a rehearsal dinner was certainly a grand affair, a sight straight out of a fairy tale—with a string quartet, tables loaded with extravagant foods and desserts, and even a champagne fountain. In fact, Mel felt like her whole life had turned into one big fantasy. She was actually sitting at a table with her fiancé, the crown prince, as his parents, the king and queen, sat beaming on either side of them.

Mel cast a glance at her future mother-in-law, who returned her smile with a wide one of her own. She looked the perfect picture of health and vibrancy. The king was equally fit and formidable. It didn't look like she and Ray would be ascending any throne anytime soon. A fact she was very grateful for. No one would ever be able to replace her real parents, Mel knew. But her future in-laws had so far shown her nothing but true affection and kindness. In fact, the whole country had received her with enthusiasm and acceptance—a true testament to the regard they felt for their prince and the royal family as a whole. And all despite Mel's utter unpreparedness for the rather bright proverbial spotlight she'd suddenly found herself in once her and Ray's engagement had been announced to the world.

Her fiancé pulled her out of her thoughts by placing a small kiss on the inside of her wrist. A sensation of pure longing gripped her core.

"I can't wait to be alone with you," he told her.

"Is that so?" she asked with a teasing grin. "What did you have in mind?"

He winked at her. "To dance with you, of course."

Mel gave in to the urge to rest her head against his strong shoulder. "There's no one else I'd rather dance with," she said, her joy almost too much to contain.

"And there's no one else I'd rather call my wife."

His words reminded her that the true fantasy had nothing to do with the myriad of parties being held for them over the next several weeks or even the extravagant wedding ceremony currently being planned. All that mattered was the complete and unfettered love she felt for this man.

Her husband-to-be was a prince in many more ways than one.

* * * * *